RUN

It's so exciting yet so nerve racking to share my first book with the world. I often feared being judged and the possibility of failure. Lisa Nichol's once wrote, "Don't wait for the fear to stop before you leap. Be willing to leap afraid." You're witnessing my jump! Thank you so much for the support! This book is dedicated to those who are on the cliff of their dreams. Those, who like me, have the habit of looking down before you leap. I encourage you to jump! If you have to, build your wings on the way down. If you fall, hit the ground running. No matter what, just keep going.

-Dria

Moments in Time

1

Invasion

His head rose quickly as the loud sounds of glass breaking woke him out of his slumber. *The fuck?* He waited until he heard a light thump before he quietly kneeled beside his mattress and took hold of his all black firearm that he kept beside him when he slept. He knew it was a rough, half dead neighborhood, but he didn't think anyone would really try him of all people. It wasn't his obvious choice of residence but given the intense need for him to remain in the shadows of the real world, he had no choice but to occupy the cramped one-bedroom space. The sound of the moving feet came closer as he stood behind his bedroom door, the gun strongly clutched in his palm, waiting for his intruder to make themselves known in his presence. He knew if he fired off any shot, it could push him further into shadow lands he was now calling home. The bronze doorknob reflected the light from outside as it turned, the bedroom door creaking open. He held his breath as the figure stepped in dressed in baggy black clothing and a mask to cover their identity. With one swift move, he clocked the invader in the back of the head, causing them to yelp and hit the floor. The sound of the him cocking the gun made the person freeze, him pressing his barrel to their skull. The person on the other side of the black steel shook terribly under him.

"Don't speak. You move? I shoot. Simple as that. Nod if you understand." Complying with him, the trespasser laid still as statue on the light brown carpet as he turned on the light, gun still pointed. "Put your hands on your head and stand up." The person groaned but obeyed his orders. Not before making a secret vow to get back at him though. His eyebrows furrowed, a sly grin and a chuckle left his lips as he watched the petite figure stand. "Oh I don't believe this...turn around." He roughly pulled mask off his wrongdoer and laughed harder as he stepped back. "I'm gettin' robbed by a bitch?"

"I ain't no bitch." She snapped at him.

"I don't know you. So that's what I'll call you." Their eyes stayed on each other and she tightened her jaws.

"I said...I'm not a bitch. You just ask my name." Her toned hardened as she lowered her hand.

"You in my crib ma. And I told you to put your hands on your head." He looked her up and down before pointing his gun back her, forcing her to place her back on her head. She was dressed in black cargo pants that were possibly two sizes too big with an oversized hoodie and gloves covering her hands and a black book bag on her back. "And if you thought you were gonna find somethin' of value here, you're sadly mistaken." She scoffed.

"Clearly." She turned her lip up at the just about bare bedroom.

"So now you wanna insult the nigga who can decide whether you live or not?"

"Ultimately, I don't think that's up to you. Besides, I wasn't trying to rob you." Her statement broke his short reign of anger. Gloves, a mask and book bag seemed like the perfect burglar's uniform to him. He would know.

"Why are you dressed like that then?" He pointed back to it with his gun before returning his aim to her face.

"None of your business... " There was a short silence in the air as he continued to review her. There was no denying that she was beautiful. Though she had on baggy clothing and her hair was a bit ruffled up, she didn't look like someone who would even be in a neighborhood like this. "You just gon keep that gun in my face? Or do we know each other well enough for a level of some respect here? I mean I am a woman."

"Respect?" He raised his eyebrow. "You came in my crib, uninvited might I remind you."

"You don't have to; I have a lump on the back of my head reminding me every few seconds." She dropped her hands again. She honestly didn't know someone lived there.

"I'm just sayin'. Respect?" He smirked. "It wasn't given to me, so why should I give it to you? Woman or not, you're the one robbin' me, remember?" She'd had it. He'd called her out her name, he was calling her a liar, and he hit her. Oh yea, she didn't forget that. Just as swift as he hit her, she pulled out her own piece that was secured nicely in her bra and put it up to his space, stepping back a few feet away from him. He backed up also as she cocked her gun. "So, you think this is how you're gonna get my respect?"

"Trust me, I didn't want to bring it to this point but obviously, you're not getting it."

"You think you a smooth bitch?"

"One," she cocked her gun, "you're gonna stop callin' me a bitch." She walked a bit closer to him. "I'm not callin' you out your name, so don't call me out mine." He chuckled.

"Lemme tell you somethin' lil lady, even if this is a shit mess of a house, it's still MY house. You sayin' I should respect you, but you came up in my crib without an invitation. You say you not robbin' me, but you fit the description of a thief. And personally, I don't like bein' disturbed in my sleep." She turned up her lip at how he rhymed his words. "Now, with that bein said, you want some respect? You gotta show me some. Put your gun down." She knew if she wanted to make it out in one piece, she needed to play the game his way, for a little at least. She slowly knelt and put her gun in front of her feet. He admired it, black like his, but a bit smaller. He pondered on what a girl like her was doing with a gun anyway. She stood back up and he nodded. "What's your name?"

"Can you take your gun out my face now?" She looked at his gun then back at him. He'd just given her a speech on respect, so she needed to see he if he were about his word. She let out a small breath as he lowered his gun, placing it on the wooden dresser next to him.

"What's your name?" He repeated.

"Nala. What's yours?"

"Cole." He stated strongly. "So, Nala, you said you weren't robbin' me, then what are you doin'?" Becoming hot from his question, Nala shifted her feet and pulled on the sleeves of her hoodie. "Just be real." Cole watched her nervous movements as her eyes wandered around the room. To him, she obviously didn't look like she was there to harm him at all and quite frankly looked a little scared. He stepped closer to her and picked her gun that was laying at her feet. Cole held out it out to her and she eagerly reached for it, but he pulled it back from her grasp. Nala calmed herself and once he could sense her eased energy, he placed the gun in her hands and went back to their unspoken but agreed upon distance. "So?" He began to grow impatient of her silence.

"I was watching this place a couple nights ago. No one came in or out of it and I need a place to stay so..." her voice trailed off as she secured her gun back in the place she had it, him catching a small glimpse of the tops of her breast.

"And why don't you have a place to stay?" He crossed his arms.

"Because...because I'm on the run." She stood tall, gripping the straps of her backpack. He could tell by her demeanor she wasn't lying, and it put him at ease.

"No shit...I'm on the run too."

2.

So, You've Met the Girl

They stared at each other as their confessions floated through the air, one waiting to see if the other would spill their reasons for running yet secretly hoping neither one would question why. Though he was trying hard, he couldn't break away his eyes from hers. He felt she was too pretty to be from Silverdale ad definitely too green to be involved in the neighborhood's drug activity.

"Well that's cool. I guess." Nala broke the intense stare to look around the room to and to avoid asking for any further details. The bedroom was small with tight corners and a mattress with no box spring under it, only two pillows and a blanket sat perfectly in the middle of the room. A little door, which she assumed to be a closet, was heavily chipped with red paint in dire need of a few new coats. No TV or pictures, but a small lamp planted in the far-left corner of the room plugged into an outlet. It remined her of her old room growing up with her mother and she started to wonder what he was even doing in a place like this. Was he alone? Her thoughts were interrupted by a loud rumble of hunger that ached her stomach.

"Woah. You might wanna take care of that." Cole spoke up.

"I'm good." She took her backpack off and unzipped it, searching for the last of a king size snickers bar she'd been snacking on for the past three days. He watched her face sink in as she slowly stopped clawing through items and sighed. She ran her fingers through her hair and shook her head at the sight at the chocolate smears one of the few shirts she had. The sweltering summer sun had melted away what was her only food for the rest of the night.

"Stay here. I'll be back." Cole tucked his gun in his waist band.

"What?"

"I don't like repeating myself." He grabbed his own hoodie off the dresser and walked out the door, closing it behind him.

"Asshole." Nala whispered.

Cole roamed the dimly lit streets with his black hoodie covering his body and face. It was muggy tonight, but that didn't stop a group of crack heads from being drunk at this hour. They anxiously giggled and danced as they waited for their turn with the glass pipe, too enticed to notice him strolling by.

"Fiend's." He shook his head as a few of them began to argue over who was next. They reminded him too many people and too many moments in time he'd rather forget. They reminded him of people he loved, his mother for the most part, who chose that dirty rock over him time and time again. They also helped remind him of his lifetime pledge to never become one of them. Cole broke away from his deep thought, realizing he was coming up on his destination. He pushed the door open and dropped his hood, happy to be greeted by cool air.

"Hey Bashi." Cole addressed the older black man at the counter.

"Wassup youngin'? Wantin' the usual tonight?" Bashi stood up from his wooden stool and walked over to the grill.

"Uh, yea, just make two of everything." Cole leaned on the white counter. The older man chuckled as he slapped four beef patties on the hot black grill.

"So, you've met the girl huh?"

"What girl?" Cole raised his thick, usually furrowed eyebrows, wondering how Bashi knew there was a girl involved in his order.

"I've seen her wandering around here a few days watching your place. The day you left for your "deliveries"," he side-eyed Cole before dropping fries into hot grease, "she came in here and bought some fruit, a granola bar and a bottle of water. The next day she came in, she barely had enough for a candy bar. Baby girl looked so desperate I just gave it to her. I tried to offer her some real food, but I guess her pride wouldn't let her take it. Mmm, mm, mm. She sat out there for hours at a time scoping the place but never did anything said."

"Well that explains a lot…" Cole felt a small amount of guilt creep into his stomach as he thought back to Nala trying to explain she wasn't actually trying to break into his place.

"And are you behaving yourself with her?"

"Introduction coulda been better but I'm getting food for her so..."

"Knowing you and introductions, I'm sure this is a better start." The both laughed as Bashi added bacon to the grill. "How'd your little "job" go?"

"I made it back and I made my money, that's all that matters." Cole shrugged his shoulders.

"If that's all that matters to you that ain't much."

"Makin' money will always be important though Bashi. I can't get around that."

"There are things in life that are more important than just makin' money Cole and in you being in your situation, I'm really surprised you haven't realized that by now." Bashi reminded him, just like he always did from time to time as he pulled the fries from the grease and placed the well-cooked burger patties and bacon on buns. "What you really need I'm hopin' you find soon."

"And what's that?"

"Well one, a better life than the one you're livin' now. One where you can go to the market and walk the streets without disguise. You can only run and hide for so long Cole." Bashi wrapped the food and placed it in a white plastic bag.

"I know Bashi, I'm workin' on it...what's the other thing I need?"

"Love." Cole laughed and shook his head.

"I think we just have a difference of opinions when it comes to that."

"That may be true," Bashi handed Cole two cool water bottles, "but I have a feeling you're gonna start to see things my way. Give it time." Bashi chuckled as Cole shoved the waters in the front pocket of his hoodie and took the plastic bag full of food in his hands.

"Whatever you say old man." Cole slid a twenty across the counter to him and headed to his house. After the short walk from Bashi's place, Cole opened the door to his bedroom and to his surprise, Nala was still there. She was sitting under the bedroom window playing some game on her phone and charging it at the same time. His presence and the aroma of the food instantly stole her attention and a smile spread across her face.

"She smiles." He set the food and drinks down on the floor, kneeling before them.

"Especially when food is involved." She put her phone down and sat Indian style as Cole pulled out the food from the bag.

"I hope you like double bacon burgers and fries." Her mouth watered as he handed over her burger and fries along with some napkins.

"Thank you." Were her last words before she began to devour the burger. It felt like it'd been years since she had a solid meal even though it'd only over a week. The melty cheese and crunchy bacon soothe her taste buds and belly. Nala shoved a couple fries into the mix and closed her eyes at the savory combos in her mouth. Cole sat quietly, taking his time to eat as he watched her slightly sway from side to side in satisfaction. He couldn't help but let out a light laugh. She opened her caught glimpse of him looking at her and became embarrassed.

"You good." He laughed. "I know what that feeling is like." She chewed whatever food was in her mouth and swallowed it, wiping her mouth with one of the brown napkins he handed her.

"This is really good. Wouldn't expect it to come out a place like this or at this hour."

"There's like this like corner restaurant around here owned by this old dude Bashi. He stays open pretty late."

"Oh, I went in there. He seems nice."

"He is. If you stick around long enough, you'll get to know him." They ate in silence for some time, Nala finishing her food first. The warm meal sat in her belly and her body thanked her for the nourishment. She looked up at Cole as he continued to quietly eat his food and couldn't help but wonder how a person can gun butt you moment but feed you the next. His aura wasn't violently intense nor icy cold, just a little guarded. That was fine with her though because she intended to stay guarded too.

"So," Cole chimed in, "I feel like I'd have a better night's sleep if I know at least who you're on the run from."

"Does it really matter to you?"

"Yea." Cole took a sip from his water bottle. "I don't wanna wake up with guns in my face cause someone thinks I kidnapped some heiress or some axe murder."

18

"Don't have an axe o that's a no. I wish I was an heiress. Hate to be a cliché damsel in distress for you Cole but I'm just a girl runnin' from a no-good man."

 "Let you women tell it, all men are no good." Cole chuckled.

"Yea well Dante leads the parade if that's the case. Dantello Pierce, that's his real name."

"How long y'all been together?" Cole asked and felt a cold shift in her mood.

"What Dante and I have is complicated. I just know I'm done."

"Guess he's not or you wouldn't be breakin' into people's cribs in the middle of the night." They both laughed and she playfully rolled her eyes, taking a drink from her water bottle.

"Like I said, it's complicated. " Cole finished his food and gathered their trash, putting it in a plastic bag.

"Well you ain't gotta worry about it for now, you're safe here. It's a shower next to my room and I think I got a shirt and shorts for you." He stood up and retrieved the items from the dresser.

"Really?" She couldn't believe his words.

"I'm not gonna feed you and send you packin' in the middle of the night. Respect." He reminded her. "You can stay for a couple days so you can figure out your next move. That's if you want." She took the clothing and towel he gave her, her back-pack and found her way into the small white bathroom, happy to find it clean and tidy. Once she showered, she dressed herself and went back into the room to find him on the bed writing in a notebook, the small lamp in the corner beaming light in the room.

"Where should I sleep?"

"Unless you find the floor or my beat-up couch comfortable, you can sleep on this side." He nodded over to his left without lifting his hand or eyes from the paper. "You ain't gotta worry, I won't try anything."

"I wasn't afraid of that." She got under the covers, turning her back to him.

"Why not?"

"My gun said so." Cole peeked over and saw the black steel of her gun in her right hand. He looked down at his gun that laid next to him and went back to writing in his book.

3.

You Can't Leave

She's still sleepin'. Cole shook his head as he shut the wooden door to his bedroom. It was a little after three in the afternoon and she hadn't emerged from her hibernation. He went back into the living room and sat on the small torn clothed couch and proceeded to watch Sports Center, turning the volume up just above a whisper. He wasn't paying too much attention to the program though, her presence clouding his thoughts. Irritated, Cole sucked his teeth as he turned the TV off and left the house, his hoodie covering his face and body as always. He kept a strong pace to Bashi's store as the sun glowed flawlessly in the cloudless sky. The prostitutes and crack heads alike stood outside under the shade of trees or their broke down porches, smoking, laughing, fighting, getting drunk, and somehow, making money. Cole never understood how they could be happy with that lifestyle. Why someone would risk their lives and the love of others for something damaging and cheap? He knew he'd never get an answer and even if he did, it would never be an acceptable one.

"Ahh, so you made it out alive." Bashi stood up from his wooden stool behind the counter.

"Yea," Cole put his hood down, " probably because she's been sleep for forever. Should I wake her up?"

"Nahhhhh." Bashi waved his hands. "She's got that good food in her tummy and she finally has a chance to get some good rest. You let her sleep."

"Bashi I'm tryna be nice but I don't really know her man. How I know she ain't some secret spy or somethin' sent here to take me down sooner or later?"

"Oh hush. Now I seen that girl. If she was a spy, she would've known when you were home instead of campin' outside with those hobos and druggies, hardly sleeping. She even came in here and fell asleep with her head on the table, but I didn't wake her. Poor baby girl." Bashi shook his head, taking a seat on his wooden stool. Cole sucked his teeth.

"You just on her side cause you think she pretty." He leaned on the counter. "She was tellin' me about some guy Dantello or Dante Pierce or somethin' like that. Says she tryna get away from him. But that's such a stupid soundin' name I don't know if I believe that." Bashi shook his head as he looked out the window.

"Oh Dantello is real. I knew his father Paulie. Paulie was part of a crime and drug crew with Christian Albertelli. They ran these streets for years, smuggling and selling drugs, money rollin' in like clockwork. Didn't matter whose lives they destroyed in the process. " Bashi sighed and shook his head, walking back up to the counter. "Guess it don't surprise me young Dante's made the choice to follow in his father's footsteps. I'd heard small whispers of him restarting his father's empire, but I didn't think it was true."

"Empire?"

The rays of the sun blinded her sight as she slowly came to, noticing Cole wasn't in his spot on the bed. Nala laid still for a few moments, thanking God that she'd made it to see another day. She especially thanked him for waking up on a mattress, under warm covers, inside a house where her every move wasn't being watch and wasn't being treat like she was nothing. Even if it was only for a moment. She raised off the bed and picked up her gun, taking notice to Cole's gun and hoodie gone along the way. She crept to the door and opened it to receive silence. She shook her head and stepped into the bathroom as she yawned, stretching her hands and gun to the sky but winced in pain from the motion. Nala lifted the shirt Cole gave her to sleep in and softly touched the round purple and black bruise on her right ribs. Her skin was tender to her own touch, still feeling the sting of Dante's blow. Cole hit like Cicesly Tyson compared to him, even with the gun. Removing her shirt only revealed smaller healing wounds across her back and mid section.

"Dante, I don't want this anymore!"

"You should be grateful to even have this position in my life. You should be grateful for the fact I'm not completely bored with you and haven't tossed your ass outside."

"Now that I'd be grateful for." Nala paced their master bedroom floor.

"What was that?" Dante took a drink from his cognac filled glass and set it on the nightstand on his side of the bed. *"If you have a problem with how I run my house-"*

"Then what?!" Nala screamed as she threw her hands in the air. "You won't let me leave! You want me to fake bein happy and I'm NOT doing it! As long as I'm around you and these miserable bitches I will NEVER be happy. I swear if it weren't for Paulie-" Dante swiftly made his way to the spot she was pacing and grabbed her by her throat with one hand. He squeezed her throat tightly in his hands and slammed her forcefully into the wall behind her.

"Bitch if weren't for MY father you would have NOTHING. You could be on the streets begging for change. Or like your mother, doin' any and I do mean anything she can to get her next fix." His hot breath burned her ear as his grip strengthened, beginning to clog the air in her lungs. She gasped and scratched at his hands, trying to pry his fingers from around her neck. "Or you could be dead." Tears rushed to her eyes as she felt her heart pounding hard and fast in her chest. She felt like Dante was actually trying to kill her and this time, she welcomed the action. Nala closed her eyes as the white light began to surround her and happily, she began to accept it. But Dante wasn't going to make it that easy for her. He let his firm grip from her neck loose and she crashed on to the floor at his feet, air refilling her lungs and tears dripping down on to her cheeks. As she cried and wheezed, a devilish grin danced across his face.

"You outta be thankful my father stepped in when he did and saved what was left of your shitty life." He bent down and gently touched her red swollen cheeks, moving some of her hair out her face and wiping a few tears. "This life you have now could be easy if you just do as I say and look at this

24

differently. Now I know this is something hard for you to understand but when it comes to doing what I say, you don't have a choice." He kissed her lips with her returning one to him. *"You have your mother to thank for that."*

Her jaws tightened as she opened her eyes, hot angry tears flowing from her red lids. She heard a small sound and immediately pointed the gun to the entrance of the bathroom. Cole raised his hands.

"Woah killer. It's just me." His eyes traveled down her shirtless body, her scratches and bruises on her ribs obvious to his sight. Her chest heaved up and down as he lowered his hands. "Did he do that to you?" She quickly wiped her wet face with her free hand, gun shaking in the other as she did so. He couldn't take his eyes off her body, in complete shock and disbelief. She slowly walked towards him and he backed up, returning his hands to the air having no idea what she was doing. He watched more tears fall before the wooden door closed in his face. He thought about knocking but let it go and walked off to his bedroom. Nala wiped her face with the back of her hands, completely mad at herself for seeming so vulnerable in front of him. She didn't want him to think she was some weak girl who liked to get beat up on. She definitely didn't want him to think he could treat her the same way. She gathered herself together and left the bathroom, prepared to get her things and leave. "What are you doin'?" He set his notebook down as she entered the room and snatched her back-pack off the floor with on hand, gun in the other.

"I think it's better if I just go ahead and go now."

"You ain't leaving." He stood up as she slipped the bag over her shoulders.

"Thank you for the food and letting me sleep here. If I had any money, I would pay you but- "

"I don't want your money. And again, you're not leaving."

"You have serious authority issues."

"And you have an obvious hearing problem. I said you ain't leaving." She scoffed and shook her head.

"Thanks again." She turned to leave but he stepped in front of her.

"Okay look, you ain't safe out there by yourself."

"And I'm safe here? In some broken down, half dead, crackhead infested neighborhood? I've lived in a mansion with bathrooms bigger than this and guards with guns to follow behind me and still never felt safe. What makes you think I'm safe here?

"Me." She stood silent as she stared at him.

"No offense Cole but I really don't know you. I trust me to take care of me." She pointed to herself.

"Okay, we got some respect now let's work on some trust. Are you working with the Feds?"

"Hell no. I don't fuck with the police." After her first physical fight with Dante, she dialed the three numbers that were designated to help those in in their time of urgency and cried for help. When she released Dante's name the man taking her information, he hung up on her. And when Dante returned to the house that evening, he made her pay a heavy-handed price for talking to them. Cole stared hard at her for some time before softening his face.

"Aight. I believe you and I trust you." He emphasized trust. "I want you to trust that even though we don't know each other too well, at least know that I wouldn't do anything to hurt you, intentionally at least." She'd heard that so many times, she was starting to believe that "Easily Fooled" was secretly tattooed on her forehead in ink only others could see. "And honestly if you left, I'd feel responsible if something was to happen to you."

"And why is that?" She raised her eyebrow at him.

"Because I know I could've helped you... Just chill." He slipped the backpack straps from her shoulders, set it on the dresser and gently took her gun from her hand. "At least for a few days. Stay here so you're not seen, clear your head and think about your next move. Trust me, I know a thing or two about runnin' from people after you. If this nigga is as bad as you say he is, chances are he's already lookin' for you."

Dantello Pierce, affectionately known as Dante, sat in his office leather chair as one of his four loyal girls gave him lip service under the white marble desk that once belonged to his father. He clutched the back of her head, pushing her mouth deeper on to his long member as he reached his peak, a sound of satisfaction as he finished. She smiled up at him before standing to her knees.

"Thank you Jade." She nodded and quietly let herself out. He lit the blunt that was resting in a black glass ashtray that sat on his desk and exhaled. "Lemme try this bitch again." He picked up the office phone, dialed Nala's number and impatiently waited for her to answer. After what seemed like endless ringing, he was led to her voicemail which only further irritated him.

"Yo Joey." He called out to his main guard Big Joey who was standing outside the office door.

"What's up boss?" Joey entered the room.

"Guess nobody's spotted that bitch around town yet?"

"Checked the places we've picked her up before, but nobody's spotted her." Dante growled at his answer. "But I'll keep lookin' and let you know somethin' as soon as I find out somethin'." Joey shut the door to resume his assignment of finding Nala and Dante went back to his blunt, pondering on if Nala was worth the trouble she was causing.

"Why not just let the bitch go?" Dante stood to his feet and paced the grand office. "Shit, I got enough girls and too much money to make to be worried about her. She's brings my stock down." Dante stroked his ego as he came to the grand portrait of, he, his father and Nala hanging up on the spacious wall to left of the desk that Paulie had done before he went away. Dante could feel Paulie's eyes watching and judging his every move, just as they did when he was around and he knew if his father were to hear the things he was saying, he'd have quite a bit to say back. *Or maybe not...* Dante thought. He'd been cutting Nala's communication with Paulie for months and made Nala stay behind the last few times he'd gone to see him, maybe Paulie didn't care as much anymore. Dante puffed the blunt as he continued to stare at the portrait of the three of them. Something in him told him he was wrong about Paulie's possible newfound stance, but he wanted to find that out for himself.

4.

Things Were Gonna Be Different

Nala tossed over on to her right side, opening her eyes and sighing. Cole took a quick glance at her then returned his attention to his book.

"Am I keepin' you awake?"

"No..." She looked around the room. She felt weird waking up in a new place for the past two days without being slapped, cussed at or surround by unwanted company. She liked where she was but didn't know how long her feeling of bliss would last. Dante was smart despite his childish antics and he had access to people and resources that could only make him more powerful. Nala shook her head. She had to find a way to make sure she would never see him again. She looked over at Cole, him deep in his thoughts as he painted them on the blue lined white paper. "You a writer or somethin?" He paused, realizing that she was the first person in a while to see him writing. "Sorry, not tryna be nosy or anything..."

"When I was in high school," he cleared his throat, "I got into a fight, fucked this nigga up bad. They said I coulda killed him so his parents took me to court but thanks to my past, they just slapped my wrist with a shit load of community service hours. I had to take these group therapy classes too. We had group discussions on what pissed us off, if we were sad, were happy, if we had relationship problems, family problem with the goal to learn how to express our "feelings" in a healthy way." She watched his hand strokes glide across the paper with ease. She looked up at him and he was smiling for a change. "I didn't talk much though, so Ms. Whitfield made me write for thirty minutes straight. Didn't matter if it was a summary of the group talk, my day, a poem, as long as I wasn't keepin how I felt bottled in." His voice trailed off slowly, as his hand stopped.

"Why did you stop?"

"My thirty is up." Cole closed his book and laid it beside him, his pen going on top of it. "So, what's keeping you up? Figured you'd be knocked out snoring." He chuckled as he got off the bed. Nala's eyes widened as the blood rush to her face, becoming hot with embarrassment and suddenly feeling self-conscious.

"I snore?"

"Nah I'm just messin' with you." He threw over his shoulder before he opened the door. She smiled as she got up and followed behind him. "But what's got you up?" He flipped on the light switch in the kitchen and opened the fridge.

"I was just thinking..." She sat down on the couch and pulled her knees to her chest, "I wonder where my mother is."

"You don't know where she is?" He closed the fridge with his water in hand.

"I don't even know if she's alive." Nala admitted. "I haven't seen her since I was fourteen. To be honest, I don't even know if I ever wanna see her again..."

Nala stormed down the steps of her school gripping on the straps of her purple backpack. "Hate this fuckin' place. I hate these fuckin' people. I hate my fuckin' life." She pressed hard on the crosswalk signal and waited, tugging at the jeans that were too small for her growing body. Once it was clear, she crossed the street and began her decent walk home, fuming that she had to tell her mother she was suspended for fighting in school. It wasn't like Erika and Bianca hadn't made fun of her torn and tight clothes, which she ignored most of the time, and it wasn't like she hadn't fought either one of them but because this time the brawl happened on school grounds, she got suspended and her mother was going to be pissed.

"Tuck ya lip in before you trip on it." KJ, seventeen-year-old high school dropout who trapped all day, called out to her.

"Get your bitch before I kill her and her minion."

"First off, I ain't got no bitch." KJ raised his hands.

"Well Erika doesn't seem to think that! They cornered me in the bathroom. First, she started with me about you and then she started goin' in on my clothes. Just sayin' foul shit about me and my mom. I can't help it if my mom is fuckin' crack head Keith and doesn't give a fuck about me." He grabbed her to stop her fast-paced walking.

"Fuck that bird. She just jealous of you cause you don't have be on your knees for someone to be willing to have a conversation with you." She rolled her eyes.

33

"And as for your mom -"

"I don't wanna talk about her." She looked off down the street shaking her head.

"C'mon Nala...you know you can talk to me."

"... she's getting worse. We don't have ANY food, they're about to cut our lights off and I know Ms. Regina cares but she's over helpin' us out on the rent. I can tell she's looking for the right time to put us out. Ma just doesn't give a damn." She started her walk again, him strolling right beside her.

"Why ain't you tell me Nala? You KNOW I woulda been took care of that."

"Because it's not your responsibility to take care of it. Besides, after tonight, none of this will matter."

"Why not?"

"Cause I'm leaving. I ain't seen my mom in days so she's probably dead somewhere this time or decided to just leave without me. I'm better off on my own anyway."

"Your fourteen and don't know shit about the streets or how to take care of yourself. Where you gon' go? How you gon' make money?" KJ stepped in front of her.

"I'll learn. You did." She stared up at him reminding him of his own come up. KJ had left the crowded three-bedroom apartment he shared with his mother and seven other siblings and made enough to get a place for himself and two of his younger brothers.

"You right but this ain't somethin' you should get into. Tomorrow morning, I'll meet you at your spot and I'ma have some bread for you."

"Keith -"

"If I had enough on me now, I'd give it to you but here," He handed her two hundred-dollar bills from his pocket, "Take one and give it to Ms. Regina. Tell her that it's from me and that I'm comin' to see her tomorrow with the rest. She knows me well. Get food and whatever you need for now with the rest."

"Thanks Keith."

"I gotchu. I gotta go make some runs though. Eight thirty La I'll be outside your crib." He stated firmly before turning to the opposite direction and walking off. She walked the rest of the way home feeling lighter on her feet, finally feeling like she had a solid plan, and everything really was going to be fine for once. Nala walked down the block to the small apartment she shared with her mother, noticing a shiny black car out front of the building. A feeling of uneasiness crept inside her body as she walked up the steps to her third-floor apartment. When she reached for the knob, it was already unlocked. She thought about leaving right then, but she was afraid her mother was back and might need her. As she entered inside, a strong cologne scent hit her nostrils.

"Don't make me do this Paulie." She faintly heard her mother plead.

"I told you if you kept this shit up, I was going to do this. Do you forget we made a deal the last time you did this?"

"I promise this time Paulie."

"Diana, I'm not doin' this with you this time! Now, where is she?" The man roughly grabbed her mother's face.

"Ma you okay?" Her mother turned around looking tired and terrified, her eyes glossy and wet.

"Wha-what are doing here Nala?" Her voice cracked. "You're supposed to be at school." Nala ignored her looking to the man in black behind her mother. He was well put together, dressed in an all-black suit with shiny black shoes to match. His face was firm, but he didn't seem to be a threat. At least not to her. "Nala?" He mother called to her.

"I wasn't feelin' too well. Momma...are you okay?" She looked back and forth between her mother and the man as he placed his hand on her mother's shoulder.

"This is a good friend of mine, Mr. Pierce." Nala stayed silent as she kept looking at the pair. Her mother's eyes focused in on the green paper in her hand. "Where'd you get that money?" She quickly snatched it from her fingertips.

"It's mine. I-I found it." She watched her mother put it in her back pocket as she sniffed and scratched at her skin. The cleared his throat and Nala's mother smiled weakly at her.

"Nala," she wiped her nose, "you're gonna go away for a little bit so that mom can get a few things done around here. Mr. Pierce has promised to take good care of you, right Paulie?" Her mother looked at the man with hard eyes.

"Of course." He smiled. "My son is going to love having you around. He'll finally have some company." Nala became scared as she gripped her straps tighter.

"I don't wanna go." The smile on his face fell.

"I know it might be an adjustment but it's honestly best this way." He stepped forward to her. She backed and let out a small sound, feeling like she hit a brick wall. She looked up behind her and a big bald man towered over her, breathing heavy out his nostrils.

"It's gonna be alright Nala, I promise. I'll come see you when you're nice and settled." Nala shook her head. She had a plan, eighth thirty tomorrow.

"I said I don't wanna go!" She raised her voice. Mr. Pierce looked to the big man behind him and then back Nala who was staring at him.

"I hope you understand that this is for you good. Now you can kiss your mother goodbye and he can walk you to the car quietly or we can go the route in which I have him drag you out of here kicking and screaming. Those are your choices. As for you going though, my dear...you don't have a choice."

5.

One in the Same

"That's kinda fucked up." Cole's voice trailed off as he looked around. He found himself back in bed, Nala laying down at the opposite end with her feet on the wall. It was late but they could hear the drunks and druggies having their nightly binge party. She stared up at the ceiling and shook her head.

"Yea kinda..."

"I know what's it's like for someone to give you up without a second thought. My mom was like that too." She sat up and moved closer to him, pulling her knees to her chest.

"You wanna talk about it?" She asked after a few moments of silence.

"Nah, not really." She understood, she knew some things were better to keep inside. Sometimes the pain is just too deep to pull out.

"You know, you never did tell me why you're running. It's got to be something big because you asked me if I work for the Feds." She let out a small laugh and nudged his arm, encouraging a smile on his face.

"Guess." He licked his lips.

"Murder."

"What?!" She raised her hands in the air.

"I mean you do have a gun and you weren't so nice to me when we first met. I still have a small lump nesting on the back of my head." She playfully rubbed the area he clocked her.

"Aye look you broke in my crib."

"How many times I gotta tell you? I wasn't tryna break in."

"Now how was I supposed to know that?" She sucked her teeth and looked away from him. "You wanna hear the reason or what?" She rolled her eyes returned her eyes to him. "Grand larceny...multiple counts of it."

"Someone likes to use their hands." He licked his lips again before a smile crept across his face and she felt warm next to him. "What'd you steal?"

"Anything I could get my hands on or anything anyone was willing to pay for. It started out with wanting new clothes and shoes but shit, it grew over time. Paintings, cars, jewelry, china sets...had some big scores. After a while it just all caught up to me." He shook his head.

"It usually does. How long you been runnin'?"

"Bout two and a half years."

"How's that even possible?" She shook her head.

"Trust me, it's not easy." He shrugged his shoulders, not really knowing the answer himself. "I spend every day of my life inside four walls, tryna stay hidden from the world. And when I do go out, I still gotta hide my face, peek around corners, look over my shoulder just to make sure nobody followin' me." He looked over at her as she stared out at nothing in particular.

"It's a whole different world when you out there by yourself." She moved her attention to him, and they caught eyes. Her eyes traveled down his face, admiring his handsome features as she went along. His beard made him look rugged and rough, but his eyes said the opposite. They drew her in. "Aren't you scared?"

"I used to be...Are you?"

"Yea." She didn't know what Dante would do this time if he were to find her.

"I know, I ain't goin' to leave you though. You gotta have me too. I can't hold you up and watch my back at the same time."

"We come with a lot shit. What's the use of adding to it?" Nala spoke up after a few moments.

"" If you want to go fast, go alone. If you want to go far, go together." It's an African proverb. Look like I said, I know you're scared, and it doesn't seem like you know what's next. I'm just sayin', you roll with me, I'll have your back. You just gotta have mine." Cole looked to her, but she was staring out blankly again. Feeling uncomfortable with her silent rejection nudged between them, he got up and snatching his pen and book off the floor.

"Where are you going?" She felt his rays of heat as she got off the mattress too.

"Away from you."

He watched his mother angrily throw his clothes, toys and any other belongings into to a large suitcase. Her hair was scattered and sweat pooled on her forehead as she rode the wave of her high. Seven-year-old Cole stood at his red bedroom door frame, crying to himself as he watched her pack his things. She'd done this many time before, but she never seemed as serious as she did now. He cried harder as she zipped up his suitcase and threw it onto the floor letting out a frustrated yell. She herself began to cry as she clutched her hair, breathing unevenly.

"I'm sorry Cole but... I just- you need to go." She sniffed, wiping her nose with her shaking head.

"Mom I don't want to go." He ran up to her and hugged her tiny waist. She closed her eyes as they sobbed together. She kneeled to his level and grabbed his light face, looking into her son's confused eyes.

"Cole, you don't understand-"

"I do!" He assured her. "Grandma tells me that you're sick and that love and prayer will make you feel better. I love you Mommy.i pray for you everyday. I promise, I will love you every day, I just want you to get better." His little mouth confessed. His tears flowed heavy as they spilled on her hands. She felt worthless as she looked into his wet, pure and honest eyes. She knew she didn't deserve him.

"I love you Cole." She hugged him for the last time as she heard the front door open. "But love," she pulled back and stared him in his eyes, "it just ain't enough sometimes." She stood up as her mother stood in the door way, Cole noticing her as well. "Let's make this short."

"No! I'm not leaving you!" Cole stood tall, clenching his fist tight. His mother picked up his suitcase and handed it to his grandmother. "Did you hear me? I'm not leaving you!" She turned around and smacked his face. His skin stung as he touched his cheek and he looked up at her stunned.

"You better watch your mouth." She pointed to him. "Take your bag to the door and wait for your grandmother." He slowly walked past her and took the heavy suitcase from his grandmother.

"Hey Grandma." He mumbled. She kissed his burning cheek and smiled at him.

"Hi honey. This is a little heavy, so I'll take it. Why don't you wait for me by the door while I talk to you mother?" He stood by the door as he listened to the two argue over his mother asking for some money to "hold her over", hate coloring his heart dark. As far as he knew, he didn't have a mother. She was *dead* to him.

6.

Early Birds and First Worms

The sun lit up the room as Nala opened her eyes and noticed Cole was still absent from his side of the bed. She turned over onto her back and sighed. She felt super awkward being there, especially since she didn't give him a solid answer on whether or not she was going to stick around for the long haul. She picked her gun up and stood, stretching her arms to the ceiling. Careful not to make any noise, she walked over to the small window in the room and peeked outside through the blinds. The streets were silent and free of the fiends that constantly occupied them. She shook her head as she stepped away from the window. Nala took her own hoodie and pulled it over her head, tucking her gun in the waistband of her sweats. She could hear the T.V. on in the living room but doubted that Cole was awake. She just wanted to go on a walk and clear her head for a moment. Nala quietly opened the bedroom door and stepped out to shut it behind her. Seeing that he was asleep on the couch and unbothered by her movements, she slipped out the front door and started towards Bashi's.

"Well look who it is." Bashi smiled as he noticed Nala coming towards him.

"Good morning." Nala returned the gesture.

"And what's a pretty girl like you doing out this early?" Bashi unlocked the doors and allowed her to go inside first. "You should be getting your beauty sleep you know?" He laughed as he turned on the lights and made his way behind the counter. "Probably that belly of yours. Have a seat, I'll cook ya somethin' up." He slapped his hands together.

"I don't have any money to pay you."

"It's on the house." Bashi gave her a soft smile as she took a seat at a nearby table. He grabbed some strawberries from a small cooler and began to cut them up. "You seem to be in better spirits since I last saw you."

"Good sleep and food will do that to you. I hope that Cole is keeping you good company. That helps too." Nala slightly turned up her mouth.

"I wouldn't say it's all that good."

"He's a hard one that kid." Bashi placed a bowl of strawberries lightly sprinkled with sugar in front of her with a cold bottled water.

"I just don't get why he has to be such a hard ass. I mean I get it but still..."

"You two just need some more time to get to know each other. You'd be surprised to find out how much you have in common." Bashi returned to the grill, sizzling noises and bacon aroma following behind shortly after. The beeping from Cole's watch woke him from his sleep. It wasn't that great of sleep anyway being that he chose to sleep on the uncomfortable and worn-down sofa. He was too stubborn to go back in the room and sleep next to her. Cole got up and brushed his teeth as he thought of the days moves. He was hoping to get another job from Don, a close running partner of his that kept him in the business of the underworld,

46

even though he was supposed to stay far away from it. As usual, Cole threw his hoodie over him head before closing the front door behind him, not even bothering to check in on Nala.

"This had to be the best bacon, egg and cheese biscuit I've ever had in my life." Nala pushed her empty plate away from her as she patted her belly. "Bashi, your talents are too good for this place. You should expand and franchise." Bashi chuckled as he took another sip from his coffee.

"That don't sound too bad there young lady. But I don't see me leaving this place. I've been here all my life." Nala looked out the window past Bashi at some junkies who were running around high, laughing and joking at such an early hour. "Don't let these broke down houses and untamed yards fool you. This place used to be alive and well back in the day. I grew up a couple streets over from this one, got my first kiss down at the park on Oakley Ave," they both let out a light laugh, "First fight, first girlfriend, first everything. This is just home for me."

"I guess I can understand that. But what about your family? I'm sure amongst all those "first time" for you there's a Mrs. Bashi."

"She was taken too soon from me..." Bashi quietly took another drink from his coffee and Nala wanted to smack herself for even saying something.

"I'm sorry to hear that Bashi..." Nala looked down at her hands.

"How about we take a walk?" Bashi stood up from the table.

"Fuck." Cole muttered to himself. It wasn't even eleven o'clock and the sun was already beaming. The sweat was beginning to gather heavily on his face, and he was all too ready to toss the hoodie off his body. He weighed back and forth the pros and cons of the action and decided against it. He couldn't take any chances. Cole finally approached the pay phone about eight blocks up from his rundown sanctuary and leaned up against it to cool down before placing his phone call. He put the two quarters inside and dialed the contact number he made sure was engraved into his brain.

"Hello?" The voice of his own personal angel sang.

"Hey Nana." He tried to keep the contagious grin from spreading across his face but no luck.

"My handsome boy! How are you Coley?"

"Aww come on Nana. Last time you said you weren't gonna call me that."

"And if I recall correctly, you said you would fit in some time to see me. That was about two months ago Coley."

"I know Nana. I keep sayin' I'ma come see you but-"

"I know honey. I know. How are you? Are you eating well and staying with the radar?" Cole smiled to himself again as he relaxed and looked around at his surroundings. It seemed as if everyone was trying to enjoy the few last weeks of summer.

"You mean under the radar. Yes Nana, I'm doing fine. I should be asking you all these questions. How are they treating you there?"

"I am doing great honey. I've been getting my behind up and taking walks with the Gerry and some of the other girls. They want me to have as much exercise as little old me can handle."

"That's great Nana. You sound good."

"And you sound a little bothered. So, are you going to tell me about her?"

"Me and the fellas used play right here on this corner and people would come by and drop coins and dollars in my sax case. Now we weren't doing it for money at first. We were just some young kids tryna stay out of trouble and not be like the rest of the knuckle heads that were runnin' around here sellin' poison." Bashi shook his head as they both stood on the empty cracked concrete corner and took in the sight of the fallen neighborhood.

"The neighborhood I grew up in wasn't this bad but I'm sure it's not too far behind it. My mom was a heavy user, if not the worst there ever was. The things you witness when your parent is a druggie, the things they do for the high...I'll never understand it." Bashi linked his arm with hers and continued their walk until he stopped in front of an all brick house with white shudders and a black gate surrounding it. The yard was clean and healthy with green grass and a flower bed filled with pink, yellow and white flowers to decorate.

49

"My wife Evelyn was a lovely woman. Came from a troubled and crazy family, even a little crazy herself but I loved her. when we got married, I hadn't quite had all the money for a house yet, so we lived with my parents. For months on end she just kept bugging me about getting our own house but not wanting to move out the neighborhood since we both grew up here. You women. You make request and right then and there do you all expect it to be done. Don't give a man no time to fulfil it." Nala laughed and Bashi shook his head with a smile. "She just about drove me crazy. But being a newly married man, my father gave me the best advice on marriage, which is keep her happy by any means. Now my plan was to get a small green house a few streets down from my parents. One day on my way to work Ms. Newman, who was eighty-six at the time said to me, "Every time your wife walks by my house, she just gets to grinnin' and smilin' at it. What's wrong with that girl?"" Bashi's broad shoulders bounced with laughter. "And I'd told her about us wanting our own place and how I was saving for the little green house. That was all the conversation we had about it. No more than a week later, Ms. Newman passed away and left the house to me and Evie since she had no children herself, paid for and all."

"That was so gracious of her."

"She was a sweet old lady. Gave us a push start to building our own family. We were both so grateful."

"I'm sure, it's such a beautiful house. I can only imagine what the inside looks like."

"It's lost its spark. I stay open so late cause I can hardly sleep in there most nights." Nala looked over at Bashi's face and could see he was holding back tears that were so desperately trying to free themselves. "I'm not sure what's worse, being the child of a habitual drug user or being in love with one." Nala looked back at the house and rested her head on Bashi's shoulder realizing that he too was a part of the abandoned.

"You almost out of here boy?" Mr. Greg called out to Bashi who was wiping down tables.

"Just about Mr. Greg."

"I don't know how you can go to work every morning yet still find time in the evening to come and help me out. Hell, I just might leave the place to you once I kick the bucket."

"Just because I have a grown-up job doesn't mean I'm too good to come and help out my favorite old boss."

"Hey now, I'm old but my old ass can still keep up" Mr. Greg slapped the counter with a laugh. " But you? You're better than me when I was your age. Got a great job, almost two years into marriage. I'm proud of you, doin' it the right way."

"I appreciate that Mr. Greg. It's been rough but I think everything is starting to level out." Bashi wiped his last table.

"You just got to keep the faith young man. How is Evie? I saw her the other day and she looked really good."

"She's excited to be starting our family. I really think we needed this." Evelyn had found herself riding the new wave of drugs that'd been flowing into the neighborhood thanks to Paulie and Christian. The pair had set up shop by the neighborhood park and it seemed like everyone wanted a piece of what they were sellin'. It caught Bashi by surprise when he found out Evelyn had been trying poison herself. She told him it helped her ease the she from them living in his parents' house but once they had finally moved into their own place, he made her promise not to dip again. She promised.

"Why don't you finish up now and go home a little early. Go love on and take care of your newly pregnant wife. I'm sure she's waiting on you." Bashi grabbed his jacket from the behind the counter and slid it on.

"You're right I should go. Same time tomorrow Mr. Greg?"

"If you want. An old fool like me doesn't mind the company." Both men exited the restaurant and Mr. Greg locked the doors as the streets began to come alive with rowdy fiends and people alike.

"You want me to walk you home?" Bashi raised his brow at the activity around him.

"I'm fine you go on. Ain't nobody gonna bother me." Mr. Greg patted the pocket of his coat. "Trust me. Hell, you want me to walk you home?"

"I'm fine." Bashi laughed. "You just get home safe." Bashi walked along the sidewalk, stepping over a needle or pipe every now and again. He started to think about the life he wanted to create for his own *family and crack pipes and fiends weren't a part of that life. He knew Evelyn loved the house and would be sad if they had to leave her family as well as his behind. But they had to. They needed to if they wanted to give their child a real chance to have a better life. Bashi was finally at his home and he took out his house keys, confident that Evelyn would want the best for them just as he did. "Evie." He called out to her once he was inside the house. The lights were on, but it was quiet. She wasn't at her usual spot on the couch flipping through the tv channels and waiting for him. "Evelyn?" He called again as he rested his jacket on the coat and hat rack by the door. Eerie silence answered him, and an uneasy chill crept up his spine. It wasn't until he turned the corner to enter the kitchen did he understand the silence. There Evelyn was, four months' pregnant face down on the floor with a needle inches from her cold grasp.*

"It sounds like she just needs a really good hug."

"I'm just helpin' out with a place to stay until she figures out what to do next. I ain't givin' out no hugs, she can hug herself."

"Now Cole, don't you go actin' like one these knuckle heads to her. If her last boyfriend was horrible in the way he treated her, why would you make it worse?"

"Nana-"

"Listen to me Cole. I sound healthy and happy and it's because I am, but I'm also tired. Every night I pray for the Lord to hold off on my homecoming

53

until I know you have someone else, besides the Lord, in this world to go through life with. Although I would like to see you in a loving union so that you can grow your own family, she could just simply be a friend. Someone to laugh with, someone to listen to your woes and understand you. Someone to get lost with and forget this stupid cruel world." Cole hated that she was right.

"I don't know Nana, that sounds like a relationship to me." They both laughed to lighten the mood.

"Some of the best relationships stem from friendship. Me and your Grandpa Moses were friends for a whole year before he made his move."

"Grandpa Mo was smooth like that huh?" He laughed again as he dropped another quarter in the machine. He listened to his Nana tell the story of her and Grandpa Moses' love adventure for the one thousandth time, but he didn't mind. It was nice to know a love like theirs was still strong even though death had parted them. It made him think of Nala. Though he hadn't known her for very long and they weren't really on the best speaking terms at the moment, the time they did spend being cordial to each other he enjoyed. It was nice to finally talk to someone other than Bashi or the four walls he was confined to. He didn't realize until then how much he missed having a friend.

7.

Surprise, Surprise

"You see for me," Bashi continued on with his street sermon as the pair walked arm in arm, "It's not about running away from the problem. It's about facing it, understanding the magnitude of it and then tackling it. You may see a neighborhood in shambles and broke down abandoned homes and the same junkies out here fightin' and carryin' on. It's true, that's what this place is." Nala peeked down an ally way to see a woman with disheveled hair take money from an equally disheveled man and pull down his pants. Bashi took her chin away from the vulgar sight and fixed her gaze onto something else. "But it's what you choose to focus on. Even when the world around you turns in to shit..." Nala smiled at Bashi's store, realizing they'd walked the whole neighborhood.

"I guess you're right."

"I know Cole isn't that easy to deal with, trust me, I've been knowing him for quite some time now. He'll soften up." Bashi unlocked the doors and let Nala in before him.

"He's a far cry from Dante that's for sure. I'm just happy to wake up and know for a fact I'm not gonna be meeting the other end of some dudes fist." Nala took a seat at a nearby booth and pulled out her phone to check for any missed calls or messages from. Nothing so far today.

"I'm very surprised that Dantello has turned out to be lower scum than his father."

"Yea well, even Paulie looks like a saint standing next to Dante. Paulie really wasn't that bad at all."

"May I ask you a question?" Bashi slid into the booth with a bowl of strawberries for them to share.

Shoot." Nala picked up the reddest, juiciest one she could find.

"What has become of Mr. Paulie Pierce?" Bashi leaned forward on his elbows.

Dante made sure his tie was straight as he waited for his father's entrance. A few years after Nala moved in, the gang was exposed. Christian Albertelli, Paulie's partner, ended up being the rat that sent Paulie to jail for the rest of his life while Christian vanished. Dante stood looking around the large cell and chuckled. Though his father was doing time for the rest of his life, it didn't seem to be extremely hard for him. White fine fabrics hung from the ceiling and a variety of comfortable plush chairs were planted throughout the spacious cell. He even had his own mini kitchen as well as an all-white porcelain tub. His father appeared dressed in all white, his black and silver strand hair slicked back to show his aging yet handsome face.

"My son." Paulie held out his arms, pulling him in to a hug.

"You're looking great Father."

"Peace will do that to you Dante." After being put away for the rest of his life for his numerous criminal activities, Paulie decided to face his own demons and revive himself to be more free thinking and positive. "So, this is a surprise."

"I just really came to see how you are. But as usual, you're doing great." Dante lied. His father sipped from his coffee cup and chuckled.

"You meet early with me just to say hello when you could have saved yourself and I more time and money by calling?" Paulie found it odd.

"Come on Dad phone calls are so impersonal. I just wanted to see you in person, talk a bit." Dante cleared his throat.

"Okay" he offered Dante a seat, taking one in the soft white chair that sat by the tub, "what's going on? Everything okay with your connections?"

"Yea everything is good. We get our first big shipment in a couple weeks so I'm a little anxious. Ready none the less."

"I understand, it can be overwhelming at times. This business takes a lot of trust and hard work. If there's any advice I could give you, it's to always trust yourself first. And be sure to have a solid team. I wish I would have." Paulie smiled raising his hands to the air. "But you should have no worries son.

"You're right Dad. Think that's what I needed to bring things into perspective."

"And how's my sweet Nala?" Though Nala didn't understand why she had to leave her mothers home, he always did his best to make sure Nala was comfortable and happy. Anything she needed or wanted, he provided because she never gave him problems and he made sure Dante treated her with respect.

"She's great. Busy as usual. We both are pretty busy these days actually."

"Too busy for me? She hasn't been to see me in almost two years. She doesn't call or around when I happen to be on the phone with you... it's not like her to go so long without talking to me. And you're sure she's not upset with me?"

"No, she's not mad at you. I hardly get to see her these days myself honestly. She's excited to be starting her new fashion line so she's devoted herself to that one hundred percent."

"My beautiful talented Nala. All this time, I thought she hated fashion. I couldn't get her to put on a damn dress for the three months she stayed with us." He laughed warmly at the memory of her. "And how is everything between you two?"

"Great." He lied.

"How great? I figured you would have proposed to her by now or I'd at least be a grandfather." Paulie shook his head in disappointment.

"Yes Dad, we're fine." Dante smiled through his lie but this time, Paulie could see it was forced. "And if you want marriage and a grandchild, you'll have to wait for her. She's very goal orientated these days."

"I suppose I'd rather her be too focused on fabrics than end up like her mother. It just doesn't make

58

sense that she would go this long without talking to me..."

"I'll be sure to have her make an appointment or call you as soon as she returns from whatever country she's decided to explore this time. She takes the jet all the time to look at fabrics, cultures, ya know, says she wants to be inspired." Dante inwardly smiled at how the lies easily cascaded from his lips he believed was soothing father's ears.

"I see... Well my son, it seems that everything is on the right course. I look forward to hearing good things from you in the next few weeks."

"Yes sir."

"Hopefully, my next surprise visit will be from Nala. Please, give her my love and be sure she calls me." They embraced each other for a brief moment before Dante was escorted out by one of the guards that was standing outside Paulie's cell. Paulie watched Dante disappear down the hallway before sitting back down in his chair to return to his coffee, replaying their conversation. Nala and fashion? That didn't sound right.

"Sebastian," Paulie called out to another guard in charge of watching his cell.

"Yes sir?"

"I need you to consider the whereabouts of Nala Wilson over the past six months."

"Sure thing. Anything in particular I should be looking for?"

"Anything you can come up with."

"I'll get right on it." The hefty guard left him alone in his chair to follow orders. Paulie shook his head once more before taking another drink.

"It's just not like her..." Dante strutted out the prison doors with Big Joey close behind him. On the outside, he was smiling but, on the inside, he was uneasy and irritated. His father seemed more interested in Nala than what Dante had been spending the last few years trying to rebuild, his father's legacy. Big Joey opened Dante's car door for him before getting in on the other side.

"How's the old man?"

"Comfortable as usual. He has those people bending at his hands." Dante looked back at the prison as they pulled off.

"He must be proud that you've taken the liberty to restart the family business."

"Yea but I'm not gonna let anyone or anything tear it down again. My father relied on a "friend" and you see where it got him. That's why I continue to be my own man. I'll be the one to bring the Pierce family name out of its shame." Dante lit up a blunt the was waiting for him in the limo's ashtray. "Now if I could just get Nala in line..."

"Did he mention her?"

"Of course he did..."Dante stared out the window as he continued to inhale and relax. He knew his lies would only hold up for so long. He needed to bring Nala to see his father soon. "Tomorrow, we start the real search. Every bus station, train station, homeless shelter and hotel with a twenty-mile

60

radius will be swept through thoroughly. She doesn't have any friends or family she could run to. She's out there alone. Trust me...she'll turn up."

Cole inwardly rejoiced when he could finally see the house not too far off his path. The sun was beyond flaming and the amount of people walking the streets were too many for his liking. He thought of stopping over at Bashi's to grab a quick bite to eat but decided against it. All he wanted to do was shower and chill for a moment. He was also hoping that Nala had woken up in enough of a good mood to accept his apology for last night's walk out. Speaking with his grandmother helped him realize his reaction to her hesitation to stay with him was a bit out of line. He let out a sigh of relief as he opened the front door, all too happy he was home and that the cool air was there to greet him. The TV was on a low mumble, just as he'd left it, yet the house was too quiet. He pulled his sweaty hoodie over his head, his shirt coming off with it as he headed to the bedroom. He opened the door to find she wasn't in there either. He furrowed his eyebrows and shut the door as the shower called out to him.

"Try not to think about it. Try not to think about anything for that matter. Just take it one day at a time and you'll know what to do." Bashi walked Nala to the front door. She was ready to head back to the house after spending just about the whole morning with him. She loved his company. He was understanding, inviting and wise.

"I will Bashi. Just need to figure how many days I have."

"Well," Bashi shrugged his shoulders, "keep in mind, how long you have, is never up to you." He pointed towards the sky. "So just take it one day at a time."

"I will." She threw over her shoulder as she started off towards the house. "Or at least I'll try." She mumbled to herself. The air was hot as Nala walked on the sidewalk under the shade of the trees. She sighed heavily, removing her hood from her slightly sweaty face.

"Ain'tchu hot?" Nala looked up to see the same woman that was in the ally sitting on a cracked step in front of an abandoned green house.

"Can't you tell?" Nala tried to be friendly as she slowed her pace.

"Hell yea, you sweatin' worse than Jamal when he's on the dust." She laughed wildly at her own joke. "I ain't seen you round here befo' and you sho' nuff don't look like you belong here either. Where you from? You pretty." Nala could see there was a pipe and needle beside the woman.

"I don't really have time to talk today, maybe some other time." Nala continued walking on.

"Well my name is Brittany so if you need to know anything round here, I'm ya girl." Brittany pointed to herself.

"I'll keep that in mind." Nala rolled her eyes and her pace quickened. A smile crept on to her face when she realized how close she was to the house. She hoped Cole still didn't have the standoff attitude he

62

was throwing her way last night. She was felt she was being completely honest with him. Him running away from the law while she's trying to get away from a possessive man would only cause them more problems. They already had enough of those. She opened the door, TV still on and no Cole in sight. "Good, I can take a shower." Nala raised her hoodie her head revealing her soaked white beater. She opened the bedroom door to grab her book bag that held her clothes and came face to face with a naked Cole. She tried to stop her eyes from looking down, but it was too late. Their eyes met briefly before she swiftly shut the door and covered her mouth with her hand. She let out a small laugh of embarrassment and pleasant surprise.

8.

For Now

Cole, fully clothed in black sweatpants and a white beater, opened the bedroom door to be met with silence again. The sink faucet in the bathroom squeaked as Nala turned it off, wiping her cool wet hands on her blushing face. Cole lightly knocked on the bathroom door and she slowly opened it.

"My bad about all that. I usually dress in the bathroom, but you weren't here so..."

"No, it's okay," Nala tried to look everywhere but at his face, "I should've knocked I guess."

"I take it this is what you came to get?" He held up her black book bag.

"Yea." She let out a small laugh and took it from his hands. "Thanks."

"So, we good?"

"We're fine Cole. A little penis never hurt nobody." His eyebrows shot up as she laughed as she shut the bathroom door and started her shower. He stood at the door for a moment or two before laughing and walking away. Nala finished her long shower and emerged from the bathroom to find that Cole had a spread at the living room for them.

"What's all this?" She unwrapped a green towel from around her hair, letting her naturally curly hair flow freely as she looked about the living room table. There was a large bucket of chicken and another bucket of fries with as much ranch and blue cheese she could possibly take.

"It's lunch, what it look like?" Cole raised an eyebrow as he set napkins down next to their paper plates. Nala smiled her way back to his room to return her book bag to its regular spot before heading back into the small living room.

"Those hot wings smell like heaven." Nala took a seat on the couch next to Cole and grabbed the remote on the other side of him.

"Yea Bashi makes the best kind. Hold up whatchu doin'?"

"I'm changing the channel, what's it look like?" She mocked him, causing a smile to creep on his face.

"Okay house rule number one: no changing channels while Cole is watching TV." He took the remote from her grip. "I know how you girls like to do." He changed the channel to ESPN to watch the highlights from the night before. Nala scrunched her nose up before taking the remote back from him.

" Never heard of that rule. You're supposed to let your guest have their choice of channels. When I leave, you can watch all the ESPN you want." She shoved a golden hot fry in her mouth as she surfed through the cable channels. The slight smile Cole was wearing began to fade.

"You still on that huh?"

"Yup."

"Be real with me though, what's so bad about staying here? I know it's prolly nothin' like what you used to, and I know I can be-"

"An ass?" Nala smiled at him before popping another fry in her mouth.

"I guess." He laughed. "But I don't think I'm that bad enough for you to not stay."

"It's not you Cole. I mean it is, but it isn't. I think you're cool, but you got your own set of shit to deal with so why add mine on top of yours? "

"You make it sound like you some kind of burden or something." Nala wiped her sauce dripping fingers with one of the napkins Cole had laid out and reached for a bottled water on the black living room table. "Cause you're not." She looked over at Cole whose eyes were fixed on the First Take debate session.

"Besides my safety, give me a really good reason I should stay Cole." Cole removed his gaze from the TV to see that she was staring at him, curious as to what he would say.

"I don't know... just reminds me of when I first went on the run. Can you imagine seeing your face on just about every TV you pass by? People doing double takes on you, squintin' at you?" He shook his head. "You realize you're by yourself. No friends, you can hardly pick up the phone and call somebody you do care about. You start to feel lonely...and empty. " Cole felt himself staring too deep in her so he reached for a few fries in the bucket and returned his attention back to the show. "It's a shitty feeling to have forreal."

"Yea but I'm used to feeling like that..."

"Who say that feeling has to last forever? You feel that way right now?" Nala had to think. Despite their few hiccups, Cole was good company and his presence was better than Dante's or being alone. Then there was Bashi. She was already planning to spend the morning with him again tomorrow.

"I'll stay, for now." She picked up a hot wing as he tried to hide his smile by taking a drink. "Under one condition."

"What's that?"

"How bout lockin' a door next time you wanna be naked and free? There's a lady in the house now."

"If I wanna walk around here in my boxers all day, I can do so, I pay the bills lil' lady." He jokingly nudged her arm "By the way, I ain't find that "A little penis never hurt nobody" line you threw out too funny." Nala burst into laughter, covering her mouth so that no chicken or sauce came flying past her lips. "Yea you think it's hilarious but that's not a word that describes me at all."

"Cole," Nala finally gathered herself, "I didn't mean it like that."

"Well how did you mean it? Cause your choice of words was all wrong. Ain't shit small over here." Nala's laughter could not be tamed. "You really think it's funny." Cole chuckled along with her.

"I'm sorry but it is a little funny."

"There you go with that word again." Cole shook his head and smiled.

"I honestly didn't mean anything by it. You just took me by surprise that's all." A sort of awkward silence sat between them. Cole tucked in his bottom lip as she flipped her hair to the side and let out a small giggle.

"Yea well I'll make sure I lock the door, so I don't scare you like that again." He nudged her arm again.

"So, Mr. I Pay the Bills,", Nala laid back on the opposite side of the couch and rested her feet in his lap, placing the bucket of fries on her own belly, "What is it that you do to get the bills paid?" She raised her eyebrow. Cole wrapped his fingers around her ankle and with his left hand reached for a fry.

"Don't worry about it. Just know we good."

"So, what am I supposed to do? Just stay here all day?"

"You were gone before me this morning, so you found somethin' to do."

"I was up and wanted to see what Bashi was doin'. Where'd you go?"

"Had to make a couple calls. That's cool, just be careful roamin' out here by yourself." Cole's curious fingertips innocently danced across her skin, a slight shiver taking hold of her.

"It wasn't like I was lookin' for drugs, I was just hangin' out with Bashi, gettin' to know him. You're right, he's a cool guy."

"Well maybe you can help Bashi out around the restaurant then, see if he has some work for you."

"I guess." Nala shrugged her shoulders. "Surprised you don't work there. Your other job must pay better if you can keep this place runnin'." Cole didn't answer her, keeping his eyes on the screen of the television. She noticed his reluctance to answering her question of he made money so she decided would let it go.

For now.

9.

Old Friends

Nala laid in bed with her feet on the wall as she played some new cooking game she downloaded onto her phone. Cole was right beside her writing in his book or at least trying to. He wrote out of habit of course but for some reason, he was at a loss for words.

"You good?" She called out to him not, not even taking her eyes off the game.

"Yea why you ask?" He looked over at her.

"Because I don't hear or see your hand moving. You got about," she paused her game to look at the time, "twenty-three minutes to go." She returned to her game.

"I guess I don't feel like writing much..." He closed his book and set it down on the floor next to him. He took another glance over at her concentrated yet soft face.

"So which kid were you in school?" She randomly asked him.

"Whatchu mean?"

"Ya know the jock, the class clown, the player." He laughed at her explanation and she joined in with him. "Don't tell me you were a nerd."

"Hell no," Cole laughed again, "I guess was the one not to fuck with."

"Sheesh." She peaked over her phone at him. "So, you've really been a hard ass all your life huh?" He moved next to her and laid down as well, taking an interest in the game had most of her attention.

"I don't mean for it to sound that way but it's true. My grandma raised me so she tried to keep me in line when she could but the older we got, the harder I got. I mean I wasn't mean to her, I was just..."

"Angry." Nala's eyes fell upon him and he fell into hers, noticing a tiny beauty mark perfectly placed right under her brow.

"Yea... Anyway," he cleared his throat and looked back up at her game, "I was always fightin'. Not that I was always lookin' for a fight, but I just didn't let anybody fuck with me. Niggas thought them crack head jokes were too funny...until I showed them one day just how funny it was"

Sixteen-year-old Cole stared at himself in the skinny floor length mirror that hung on the back of his bedroom door, taking in his outfit of the day. A white off brand polo shirt with a pair of dark jeans that may have been a size or two too big for him and a pair of beat up black Converse's. Though his polo shirt wasn't name brand like the other guys at school, he knew his grandmother did the best she could, so he did his best to be appreciative. Cole picked up his backpack and exited the room he occupied in his grandmother's apartment. She sat at the kitchen table watching the news with a bowl of oatmeal and berries, the faint sound of gospel music coming from her room. Cole leaned down and kissed her forehead.

"Morning Nana."

"Well good morning to you Coley." Cole grinned at her and shook his head.

"C'mon Nana. You said once I started high school you were gonna stop callin' me that." He grabbed a Pop-Tart out of the wooden cabinet next to the stove.

"I know I know but every morning I look at you I just see my sweet little grandson. I guess you're right though, you are growing into a man." He took a seat next to her at the small white kitchen table, still having a few minutes before he had to leave to catch the school bus. "Gonna have a better day today?"

"That's always the goal."

"Good, cause I can't take much more of those of the phone calls from your principle about you fightin' or almost fightin' at school. You've been doin' this for years and I figured you would grow out of it, but it just keeps going. You can't let those boys get to you Cole. People will always have something to say."

"But they keep talkin' about Ma though. I can't just let them disrespect her like that, with the other kids laughin' and shit-"

"Cole, your mouth."

"I'm sorry Nana but you don't hear what they say to me. And the more I don't say anything the worse it gets so I ain't gon' keep lettin' it slide."

"You know," she pointed her red colored nail at him, "I outta slap you in your mouth for using that language with me but since you need to catch your bus, hear this. Your momma's battle is not yours to fight. I know words hurt and I understand that's your mother but honey, you can't go round fightin' every person who has something to say. You'll be fightin' all your life then baby." She gently rested her hand on his light face, seeing her daughter in his dim eyes. "You understand?"

"Yes ma'am...I gotta go," He stood up and placed his backpack over his shoulder, "I'm sorry for cursing with you Nana...it won't happen again." He kissed her forehead again before rushing out the door. She wiped a small tear in the corner of her eye as she stared at the door.

"Lord Almighty in heaven, please walk with my grandson..." She started to pray.

"Damn nigga I thought you wasn't gon make it." Cole's best friend Mitch slapped hands with him as the pair met at the school's entrance and walked inside the school. Mitch was tall and built for his age, his love for football contributing to his chiseled statute. The girls swooned over his brown skin and long perfectly cornrowed braids, but he hardly paid any of them attention.

74

"C'mon man you know how my bus driver is. That nigga is always late." They stopped at their lockers before first period began.

"Yo you thinkin' about tryin' out for the basketball squad? You know you got the handles for it."

"I might. Haven't really thought about it." Cole shoved a few books and his book bag inside the slim red locker before shutting it.

"Well I've thought about it and I think you should do it. You know you nice! Plus, us together? Me on the field and you on the court? We can really take over this school." He laughed. "And you never where it could take us. D-1 colleges, even to the league. Shit I'm down for whatever gets me out this place."

"Yea it sounds good." Junior Kayla Smith was strolling down the hallway like the popular princess she was with her two loyal best friends and fellow cheer mates, Morgan and Veronica, when their eyes met. He nodded his head to her, and she waved, flipping her back length brown hair before stopping at her own locker.

"Don't even go there." Mitch warned him, catching the exchange between the two.

"It's not me, it's her. She's the one with hot shot senior boyfriend but steady lookin' at me all the time."

"That's what girls do. They play mind games." Mitch closed his locker and pointed to his temple. "And your shot is way hotter than his anyway, so you need to try out man, I'm tellin' you."

"Aight nigga I hear you. I'll think about it more."

75

"Nah I need to hear you gon do it."

"Do what?" Kayla came up beside Mitch. "I hope you're tellin' him he needs to try out for the team. I've seen you play, you're pretty dope. Plus, some key players have are leaving soon. We need those spots to be filled with the best."

"And only the best." Morgan chimed in.

"She's right." Veronica popped her gum.

"Y'all bout to start a campaign for me or somethin'?" Cole laughed as he leaned up against the lockers.

"if that's what it takes." Kayla smiled. The others began another conversation amongst themselves and Cole was halfway listening but was giving most of his attention to Kayla. She was giving it right back. The sound of the bell broke their flirtatious gaze, Mitch stepping in front of Cole to hug Veronica.

"We'll catch y'all later." Mitch tossed over his shoulder as he and Cole walked the halls to their first class of the day. Time went on and before Cole knew it was lunch time. He was thankful no one had said anything slick to him, not even a joke about his clothes. It felt like a good day for once. Mitch let Cole know in passing that he needed to stop by the gym first before they headed to lunch so Cole decided to grab the books he would need for his last few classes.

"Why you always by yourself?" Kayla snuck up next to him as he was placing his books in his locker.

"I'm not always by myself. Mitch is usually somewhere next to me with a football clutched in his hands. Don't you usually have two minions trailing behind you?"

"Morgan and Veronica are my friends Cole, despite what people may think or say. So, Mitch is the only one cool enough to hang out with you? You don't like the rest of us or somethin'?" she teased.

"Maybe y'all who don't like me. Not that I care though." Cole made sure throw in. "Not all of us are so privileged to be as popular as you Miss Smith." Kayla turned her lip up.

"Trust me, most of it is unwanted attention... I'm sorry about your mom." Cole shook his head and closed his locker, leaning up against it.

"It's aight."

"It's not. I hear what people say sometimes... Half the jack asses that talk that shit to you ain't gon make it outta here anyway. They'll be the ones dealin' or doin'. Don't let them get to you. Best way to show them is by showin' out on the court but that's just my opinion."

"Y'all so pressed for me to join this team man." Cole blew out air.

"I'm NOT pressed, I just know potential when I see it."

"Oh, is that why you stay lookin' in my direction?" Cole pushed himself off the lockers and licked his lips. She blushed but looked away from him so that it wasn't too obvious.

"I don't be lookin' at you, you stay lookin' at me."
She stared back up into his brown glistening eyes
and he took in the smell of the girly perfume she
was wearing. She smelled like cotton candy.

"If that's what you wanna call it ma. But you might
wanna chill. Your man don't like me that much if
you haven't noticed." Kayla rolled her eyes as they
made their way to the cafeteria.

"Denzel doesn't like anything or anyone, not even
himself. Pay him no attention."

"He likes you though."

"I guess."

"You guess?"

"Denzel is cool and all he's just an ass sometimes.
Well, most times now..." Kayla shrugged her
shoulders, peaking down at the picture of her
placing a kiss on Denzel's cheek after the team won
the championship game the year before. With him
graduating in the spring and getting noticed by
college's around the country, she felt her place in his
life slowly fading.

"You ain't tellin' me nothin' I don't know. But if
everybody else around here treats you like you a
princess then he should be doin' the same." They
finally made it to the cafeteria where their
respective crews were waiting for them. Kayla's
royal cheering squad to the left and Cole's lost kids
to the right.

"Last time I'll mention it," She turned to Cole after
waving to her table of friends. "You're better than
some of the guys who've been playin' since

78

freshman year and I think it's time you show people." Denzel, Kayla's boyfriend, was not too far away to see the pair exchanging words as he stood in the pizza line. Kayla tossed her hair over her shoulder, seeming to be passionate about whatever she was saying to Cole. Denzel hopped out of line to find out what it was. "Promise me you'll tryout this Friday? Pretty please?" she stared up at Cole with a smile.

"Aight fine. I'll-"

"Wassup over here?" Denzel's arm slithered around Kayla's shoulders and he placed a kiss on her cheek.

"I was just tellin' Cole how the squad needs his talent this year if we want to keep that championship title." Denzel sized Cole up.

"You? A player on MY squad?" Denzel laughed as Kayla rolled her eyes and shrugged Denzel's creep arm off her shoulders.

"Ya know, we don't win games with just your points."

"Most of my points are our score but you might be too busy tossin' pom-poms in the air to realize that. And I'll be damned if I let a nigga like him walk onto my team."

"A nigga like me?" The cafeteria's noise fell to a buzz as the students realized a confrontation was brewing right in front of them.

"Don't start Denzel." Kayla warned him.

"Why you talkin' to this fool anyway?" Denzel scolded Kayla. "Look bruh, we don't need you.

Instead of worryin' about makin' the team and bein'
up in my girl face, you should be worried about your
moms." An "ooh" oozed from the crowd, anger
quickly filling Cole.

"What was that?"

"Denzel, just stop." Kayla tugged at his arm.

"I said you should be worried about your cracked-
out moms. I saw her down on 43rd and Grant Ave
givin' the meanest dick suck to-" Before the rest of
Denzel's story could even leave his lips, Cole fist
knocked Denzel to the ground. The students
whooped and hooted like animals as Cole's fist flew
high into the air before crashing down onto Denzel's
face, showing him no mercy. Denzel was trying his
best to get Cole off him or even connect a hit but
Cole's strength, powered by anger, was too much to
handle. Cole saw nothing but red as he continued to
strike and without thought laced his hands around
Denzel's neck.

"Cole, stop! You're gonna hurt him!" He heard a
voice shout out to him, but he couldn't stop himself.
He squeezed harder on Denzel's throat as Mr. Ferris,
the hefty school appointed security officer, pushed
through the excited crowd. After a few hard tugs
from Mr. Ferris, Cole's fingers finally slipped away
from Denzel's neck and the noise growing louder
around him as he came to.

"That crazy motherfucker just tried to kill me!"
Denzel yelled out as Kayla ran to his side.

"I'll kill you foreal next time!" Cole threatened
viciously as Mr. Ferris held him up against the wall
with one arm to his chest.

"Look at me Cole! Come on, Cole snap out of it!"

"They went from callin' me Crack Baby Cole to Crazy Cole. That didn't make it any better, but hey, at least nobody fucked with me after that." Cole ran his hands down his face as Nala rubbed his resting head that was now resting in her lap. "I sat in the principal's office, hands in cuffs while they waited for my grandmother and the police to show up. Couldn't even look her in the eye that day..."

"Is she still alive?"

"Thank God. I don't know where I'd be if she wasn't..."

"So, does she know her precious grandbaby likes to take things that don't belong to him?" She teased, gently tracing his hairline with her fingertips.

"Yup," Cole closed his eyes as her touch soothed him, "And she still loves me."

"As she should..." Nala looked over to see Cole's gun next to his book on the floor. "How exactly did you get into being a thief?" Cole got up off the bed and Nala followed his steps out of the room and into the kitchen.

"I made a few homies in my anger management class." Cole opened the refrigerator door and grabbed two water bottles. "It was me, Rell and my nigga Khalil. We went from stealin' chips and shit out the corner stores to clothes at the mall to just straight runnin' up in people's cribs. Khalil got us all started so I blame him." Cole laughed as the memories began to pour in. Nala took the water bottle with a smile and hopped on top of the counter.

"Boy's, y'all lifelong friendships from doin' fuck shit." They laughed loudly together as Cole leaned up against the opposite counter.

"Yea we were some knuckleheads, but we had each other's back. Khalil was bout the money, always had a score for us. Rell was always crackin' jokes, always talkin' shit."

"So, what happened to your friends?" Cole chugged from his water bottle and licked his lips to catch some water that escaped. Nala tingled a bit.

"Rell was murdered in a drive by shootin' on his block, wrong place wrong time type of shit." Cole shook head and he finished his water. "And I'm not sure where Khalil is…"

10.

Where's Yo Prince?

The sun was peeking over the horizon as Cole laid on his back and stared up at the ceiling, Nala sleeping comfortably next to him. He looked at his watch, thirty minutes before he needed to be out the door to meet Don at their usual meeting spot to discuss their next job. He always found it hard to sleep the night before he got the info for a job. He didn't want to take the wrong job at the wrong time. He knew they probably had his cell warm and waiting for him. Nala adjusted in her sleep, turning over so that she was facing Cole. Cole looked over at her smooth peaceful face, admiring all of its features. From her long lashes to her small slightly pointy nose that was home for four maybe five freckles, down to her plump lips. He couldn't imagine or understand why anyone would mistreat or put bruises on a face like hers. Though he never brought it back up, the image of her scratched and beat up on body was something he was having a hard time forgetting about. He made a silent promise to deliver a grade A ass whooping if he ever came face to face with Dante. Cole quietly removed himself from the bed and headed to the bathroom to freshen up. After, he returned to the room and grabbed his hoodie, taking another gaze at her. He kneeled on his side of the bed and gently shook her.

"What's wrong?" she raised her head up.

"Nothing. I just wanted to let you know I have to head out for a while. I probably won't be back til it's almost dark." She nodded her head before setting it back down on the bed.

"Where are you going?"

"Don't worry your sleepy little head about what I'm doin'." He chuckled and moved some hair out face. "Just know I'll be back. I'll bring dinner too."

"I've been meaning to talk to you about that." Nala yawned as she sat up and rubbed her eyes. "I love Bashi's food, but we need a better diet. Home cooked meals ya know? Preferably me doing the cooking." Cole's watch beeped at him, notifying him it was time to get a move on with the day's task.

"I hear you, we'll talk about it later. Go back to bed." She smiled and returned back to a comfortable sleeping position and he tucked her in.

"Be safe." She called out to him before he shut the bedroom door.

Dante stood behind his white marble desk and sipped from his morning cognac drink as he listened to the news. Paige entered the room in a lilac colored baby doll nighty with a breakfast tray in her hands. He looked up at her with a smile.

"Good morning."

"Good morning Dante." she returned a sweet smile as she set the tray in front of him and kissed his lips. "How are you this morning?" He sat down and she placed a white cloth in his lap.

"Just a lil' irritated."

"Tell me all about it baby." She began to massage his broad muscular shoulders as he began to cut up his steak and eggs.

"I have to take time out of my schedule to play hide and seek with Nala. It's a waste of time."

"I've been tellin' you this." Paige rolled her eyes.

"I know."

"So why waste your time on her baby? You have me," she placed a sweet kiss near his ear, "Natalia and Jade. There's also the new girl, Sasha. You don't need Nala."

"She's important to me. Not that the rest of you aren't but she and I have history. It's not that simple to just let her go." He spoke in between bites.

"If ask me, I say you let the ungrateful bitch go. Let her see how harsh this world is without you. I mean c'mon baby, a wonderful house, great gifts and shopping sprees. And of course, the best part, you." She giggled moving her hands down his bare chiseled chest. "All this and what is it that you ask of us? To be respectful of you and your house and be loyal. She's none of that baby and you don't deserve that kind of treatment." Dante took the clean napkin from his lap and wiped his mouth, pushing his half-eaten plate away after.

"So why don't you show me what I deserve then. " A smirk took hold of her face as she came from behind his chair and kneeled in front of him. Dante tossed his head back and closed his eyes as Paige did all she could to make Dante forget about Nala. His eyes fell on the picture of Nala smiling that was in a gold frame hanging up over the fireplace of his father's office. The grin on her face seemed to taunt him and laugh at the fact that she was winning their cat and mouse game. He laid his head back on the plush chair as Paige's warm tongue continue to massage him and started to think of how to back in the lead...

"Hey there Bashi." Nala smiled as she walked through the doors of Bashi's restaurant.

"Well hello pretty girl." He wrapped his big arm around her shoulders. "I was wonderin' if you were gonna come keep me company today."

"Of course!" She sat down at one of the tables and Bashi presented her with a bowl of fresh fruit and raspberry tea. He took a seat in front of her with his own cup of coffee, plain bagel and newspaper. Nala smiled to herself as she moved the fruit about to eat the blueberries first, thinking of how sweet and gentle Cole woke her just to tell her he was leaving. Bashi watched her over the rim of his glasses.

"What's with that smile?" Bashi inquired.

"What smile?" She tried to play it off.

"Oh it's too late now little lady." Bashi chuckled and Nala cheeks became hot and rosy. "I know that kind of smile anywhere. I take it you and Cole -"

"Are just friends."

"Oh now y'all are friends?" Bashi teased her a bit. "I told you, you two had some common ground."

"You were right, he is pretty cool." she admitted. "May I ask you a question?"

"You may." Bashi looked up from his paper.

"Cole left early again this morning. You know where he went?" Nala raised her brow at Bashi as he drank from his black coffee and went back to his newspaper.

"I could guess a few places but I'm not too sure." They sat in silence for a minute or so as Nala thought of how to approach the topic of Cole's employment.

"You seem to know Cole the best."

"Cole knows me best too. Almost a full year come this fall."

"He's been here a whole year?" Nala's mouth fell open.

"Yes mam, does pretty good for somebody hidin' from the law." Bashi's shoulders moved with his booming laugh.

"I know! He's really smart to be hidin' out in a place like this too. His house isn't necessarily a bad lookin' house but a few new coats of paint and some intense remodeling on the inside."

"Since you're stickin' around, you should put your own little touch on it. I'm sure he won't mind."

"To do that I need money and I'm fresh outta that." Nala went for a juicy peach slice. "Cole is Mr. I Pay the Bills so maybe he'll slide me some." Bashi said nothing as he continued to read. "It just baffles me that he even has cable. How does he pay the bills without them tracing his name?"

"The man's a mystery." Bashi folded his newspaper and got up from the table with his coffee, leaving Nala to wonder if Cole's job was a secret that he kept to himself or just a secret he kept from her.

Cole removed the hood from his head once he stepped into the cool and quiet laundry mat. He nodded over at the woman who was working at the front and she smiled at him. He took a newspaper off the top of one of the washing machines and found Don in front of the dryers bobbing his head to whatever song was blasting in his earphones. Cole took a seat two chairs down from Don and Don pulled one earphone out.

"Wassup witchu bro?"

"I'm good, stayin' low as usual." Cole opened the newspaper and pretended to read. "What's good with you?"

"Same shit foreal. Pickett got word that those Bailey Estate cribs up north got some high-profile residents I'm tellin' you man, we hit one of those and we'd be set for a while."

"Yea but you know we need a third person for those kinds of jobs, which mean two things: we gotta split more money and I have to trust them. You know I don't trust nobody but you and Pickett when it comes to this shit."

"But the bigger scores we hit, it's not gonna matter how much we split. We'll be gettin' that paper."

"The money ain't what I'm worried about nigga... What's in the paper today?" Cole continued to fake read on and Don bobbed his head as he placed a magazine on the empty chair between them.

"Langston Lofts." Cole picked up the magazine and opened it to the page Don had placed the photographs he'd taken of the area. "It's about three hours out. Built sometime last year and the rent go for twenty-five large a month. Plenty of nice cars comin' in and out the parking lot so if we don't find anything valuable? I ain't afraid to take one of them motherfuckers." Cole chuckled as he looked through the pictures. "So, you down for this one?"

"When?"

"I'm still waitin' on a connect about the security and camera systems so in a day or two." Cole nodded his head and closed the magazine.

"Yea I'm in. I'll hit you tomorrow." Cole placed the magazine back on the middle seat.

"Cool. There are things much bigger that Langston Lofts. Like Bailey Estates. You should think about that third person for real."

"I'll call you." Cole stood and threw his hoodie back onto his head and Don replaced the earphone back in his ear.

Nala said her goodbye's to Bashi to head home and nap before Cole came back with dinner. The conversation between her and Bashi had become awkward after she inquired about Cole's job. He seemed a little distant. She decided she was going to make it her mission to find out what he does, one way or another.

"You sho'nuff look like you got a lot runnin' through yo brain." Nala shook from her thoughts to see Brittany sitting on the curb smoking a cigarette. She was wearing an extremely dirty white tank that was loose on her thin body, dark blue jeans with holes and sequined pink slippers. Nala recognized it was the same outfit she was wearing the first time they met.

"Nah not really. Just hot as hell."

"Tell me about it. The last time it was hot like this, we all got as much dope as we could and went to Harvey's house to get high, he's got AC. Why come I never see you outside? You should come party with us." Brittany puffed from the cigarette between her dry fingers.

"Us?" Nala avoided her question.

"Yea! My boyfriend Jamal and Kiki and everybody else. I mean Jamal isn't just my boyfriend, he's Kiki's too! So if you want to you can talk to him or borrow him or shoot up with him, he loves to share." She scratched at her arm and sniffed.

"No thank you."

"Is it cause of that tall light skinned dude who always walks around angry and never wants to let nobody hold nothin'? Is he yo man?"

"I'm not sure who that is but-"

"Well where you stay at? Cause he's the only other fool besides that fat guy who owns that store or restaurant or whatever the hell it is, who's dumb enough to stay round here and not get high. Matter a fact, I bet you not even from round here! I bet you

90

come from some far away palace on the other side of town. You look like a pretty princess. Ya know, without the make-up and the fancy clothes and a big mansion and money. You on't even got no prince. Where's yo prince?" Brittany started to laugh uncontrollably as she scratched harder. Nala turned her back and continued to the house, leaving Brittany to ride her high wave. The way she laughed and tore at her skin reminded her of her mother. Nala quickly tossed the thought of her mother out her head once she reached the house, Cole still away. She removed her hoodie and plopped down onto the couch. Her phone rang in her pocket and an instant feeling of anxiety came over her. She removed it from her hoodie's pocket and raised a brow at the unknown number. She answered it but said nothing. The line was quiet for a few seconds as she waited for whoever was on the other end to start talking.

11.

Lie to Me

"Don't take this the wrong way but you're a lot smarter than what I thought you were at first. "Not speaking unless being spoken to first was the first thing I learned out on my own. Saves you a lot of trouble." Nala released the breath she was holding in her chest and smiled.

"I thought you might've been Dante."

"Thank God I'm not huh?"

"Yea. How'd you get my number?" Nala peeked through the blinds in the living room to see what some noise was outside. It was Brittany and her "party" crew walking past the house laughing and pushing each other as they made their way down the street.

"I snuck it out your phone last night, hope you don't mind."

"There you go again, taking things that don't belong to you." She smiled and sat back down on the couch.

"Yea whatever. As long as you're around I gotta have a way to get at you when I'm out." Cole laughed, looking about at the people coming in and out of the grocery store. "I believe you said dinner was on you tonight so whatchu cookin'?"

"Mmm I'm in the mood for some pasta." Nala told him a list of all the ingredients she would need. He went over them to be sure was not to miss anything. "Make sure you get rigatoni noodles, not spaghetti noodles."

"Yes ma'am." He chuckled. "Bashi let me hold his whip today so it won't take me too long to come home." Nala tipped her head in confusion.

"He did?"

"Yea. He doesn't let me use it often but when I told him you wanted to cook, he was down for it. Anyway, the longer I stay on here with you, the longer I have to wait to eat so I'ma get off here. I'll be back soon."

"Alright be careful."

"I always am." They hung up and Nala tossed her phone beside her. Bashi didn't mention he spoke with Cole or let him borrow his car. Hell, she didn't even know he had a car.

"Why would Bashi lie to me period?" Nala said aloud to herself in a disappointed tone. Just then Nala's phone vibrated, revealing that a new text message was available for her to read. The name displayed chill down her spine and caused her hands to become clammy. Fingers shaking, she picked up the phone and opened the message.

I know that things have been rough lately. I have been more than unkind to you. For that I am sorry. There are no words that can describe how much I miss you and how saddened I am by your absence. Please Nala, come home so that we can really talk and make things right. If you're not coming home right away, at least let me know you're safe. I love you... Dantello

"Hi how are you." The cashier smiled at her target as he put his items on the conveyor belt. Cole looked up at her briefly and gave her a head nod.

"Hey." He turned his attention back to the checkout monitor. She began to ring up the items and pass them down to the bag boy who looked every ounce of bored.

"This is a lot of food." She stated with hope of catching his attention.

"Yea a little bit."

"Cooking for your wife and kids?" He grinned, finally lifting his face to hers. *Well, well...look who I finally came across.*

"Nah just me."

"Sheesh, single, no kids and can cook? Where you been hidin' at?" He answered her question with a small chuckle as she hit the total button keeping her smile. "Eighty-three sixteen... So, you really mean to tell me a handsome man like you is going to eat alone?"

"Seems that way." He reached in his pocket and handed her a hundred-dollar bill.

"That's a shame." She touched his hand gently as she slipped the bill from his fingers. "I'm Gloria." She gathered his change from the register.

"Anderson." He lied, shoving the change into his pockets.

95

"You sure you wanna eat alone tonight? I promise I'm great company." She smirked, looking him up and down. Cole looked over at the bag boy who seemed annoyed with her trying to carry on a conversation and then back at her.

"Maybe another time Ms. Gloria. May I borrow him for a second?"

"Uh, sure have a good day. Make sure this doesn't turn into an extended break." She gave the bag boy a stern look before she went on to the next customer. The young white man looked nervous as he placed the last of the bags in the cart and followed behind Cole out the store.

"Over this way." He led him to the side of the building where he parked the car where no cameras were present. "What's your name lil homie?" Cole popped the trunk.

"Johnathan." They began to put the bags inside.

"Looked like you could use a break from bein' in there."

"Man, if I could take a permanent break from place I would. But my dad's the manager and he's all about working hard to earn money for the things you want. Been working here two years now and still don't have a brand-new Camaro."

"It'll come to you, just keep workin' at it."

"That's what I keep hearin." Jonathan pulled a carton of cigarettes from his pocket and lit one. "But my best friend is sellin' packs of work, gettin' that real money. Makes me feel like a sucka or some shit. Like I'ma turn into my old man if I keep this shit up."

"Just cause you see them gettin' money like that don't mean nothin'. At least you know you won't be the sucka in jail or dead over some work. Trust me."

"I guess." Jonathan shrugged his shoulders as puffed hard. "Anything is better than here though. And ever since ol' girl at the register started, everything's been so tight around here."

"She looked new. When she start?"

"Probably like a month or two but she's not ever a real cashier. My dad said he ain't allowed to talk about it." Cole took another hundred out his pocket and held it up.

"Pops ever slip up at the crib?" Johnathan looked around and took the money.

"He said there's some big-time thief on the run and he could be in the area but they're not really sure. Just goin' off a hunch. My mom totally freaked when she found out they were picking our store for sting operations." Cole kept his composure as he listened, making sure to pay attention to every detail. "He been on the run a minute though. Two years or some shit like that. Wish I knew him, could use the tips on how to disappear." Cole chuckled and shook his head. "Anyway, I gotta go before my Pops come out here. Last time I went missin', he caught me out back behind the dumpster smokin' weed with my girlfriend. Got grounded for a whole month. Life's a bitch without pussy." He dapped Cole up.

97

"Yea you better get back."

Cole opened the door, hauling in all the groceries, the house too quiet and dark for him. He sat the bags next to the door and flipped on the light switch, still not seeing or hearing Nala. *Man I hope she ain't leave.* He slowly opened the door to his room. And his face lit up at the sight of her sleeping on his side of the bed. He shut the door softly and went back to putting away the groceries. *She can cook whenever she wants, I just want her comfortable.*

"Why didn't you wake me up when you got here?" Nala emerged from the bedroom rubbing her eyes.

"I ain't wanna bother you. You okay?"

No. "Yes." He set down the bags in his hands and picked up her chin.

"You sure?" He stared into his face, seeing a different Nala from the one he spoke to this morning.

No. "Yea... are you okay?"

No. "I'm cool." He pulled her close and hugged her tightly. She didn't hesitate to hug him back, she needed one. Little did she know, he needed one too.

She watched him as he pushed a cart full of canned goods along the aisle, stopping to rotate and restock empty spaces. She was happy the young man took her targets invitation to walk outside with him, but she had to move on to her next customer, so she never saw the direction they went off to. *There's no way this dipshit kid is gonna give me anything that'll give me a lead. But I gotta take this chance. Lord knows I need this.* When she started out investigating the petty thefts that were plaguing the town of Harington, she didn't think years later she'd be chasing after one of the most wanted yet handsomely conniving larcenist in the nation.

"Johnathan, right?" She smiled walking up to him.

"Yea." He side-eyed her then went back to his job. "Gloria?"

"Actually, I'm not supposed to tell you, but my real name is Vanessa."

"And why can't you tell me your real name?" He pushed the cart further along the aisle.

"I'm pretty sure you know my services here are only temporary. I'm a detective. I've been looking for someone for a really long time and I think he may have come here today. You went outside with him, remember?" He pretended to think as they strolled along the aisle, but he knew exactly who she was talking about.

"Yea, I remember."

"Any reason you can think of why he wanted you to go out there with him?"

"To help him with his bags. I am a bag boy. Well, sometimes." He rotated and stocked cans of vegetables.

"Well did he make any small talk with you?"

"Not really." Jonathan shrugged.

"Okay what did his car look like?" She quickly fired back with another question.

"Look lady if it wasn't a Camaro, I don't remember what anyone is driving. Why do I feel like I'm being interrogated? If you're so sure it was him, why didn't YOU follow him outside?" She stepped in front of the cart and pushed it back with her hand.

"Just answer my question." She stared at him.

"I told you, I don't know. All I did was put the groceries in the trunk and bounce."

"That's it?" She raised her eyebrow.

"That's all I get paid for. Now if you done playin' detective, I gotta get back to doin' my job. I don't have the luxury of my "services" being temporary." She slowly let go of the cart and stepped aside, letting him past.

12.

The Makings of a Princess

"This looks...amazing." Cole sat in his seat stunned as Nala placed a plate decorated with garlic bread next to the big bowl of spaghetti and sausage covered in melted mozzarella and parmesan cheese.

"It tastes even better." Nala took a seat as well. Cole reached for the big bowl of noodles and placed a heavy amount onto his plate. After, he exchanged the bowl of noodles for the plate bread with Nala. Once his plate was made to his liking, he took a bite and let out a satisfactory moan. "Told you." She grinned before taking a bite of her own meal.

"I think you should give me a longer list next time I go to the store. This is good. How'd you get your skills?" Cole took another bite.

"I had to learn once my mother started gettin' really bad. If I didn't cook, I didn't eat." Nala shrugged her shoulders. "But when I moved in with Paulie, I had more than enough food. All the snacks, cereals, fruits you name it. Hell, even bougie food like filet mignon and duck."

"Sounds like it wasn't that bad being there."

"It wasn't when Paulie was around. He always treated me like I was his own...."

Hot rage filled tears cascaded down young Nala's cheeks as she stared hard at Paulie who was on the phone on the other side of the spacious all black limo. She looked to the husky bald guy who sitting next to Paulie as still and silent as stone, wishing she had his strength to crush Paulie's face into the window. She and Paulie's eyes met as he finished his call and her jaws clenched together.

"I know you're upset."

"No shit." She scoffed.

"That language should not be coming from the mouth of a young lady such as yourself." Paulie drank from his crystal dark liquor filled glass. "But I understand. Look where you come from."

"Where I come from?" Nala repeated with a huff. "You don't know shit about me."

"I know more shit than you think." Nala shook her head as looked out the window and wiped her tears. Her mouth almost fell at the sight of the numerous grand style mansions they were driving past. Closer to the window she moved, completely forgetting that she was with strange men and instead focused on her beautifully strange and unfamiliar surroundings. She knew they were nowhere near her old neighborhood by the looks of the luscious green lawns and fountains planted along delicately crafted stone walkways and driveways with cars she'd only seen in music videos parked out front. Some houses had a pool and tennis court, others had colorful gardens that were being tended to by workers. The longer they kept driving, the fewer houses she saw. The limo driver slowed up as he approached a long

black gate, pressing in a code then proceeding through it. The limo finally stopped, and the big bald guy exited the limo, leaving her alone with Paulie. Her hearts pace quickened as he finished off his drink. "Once we exit, you're not going to run, scream or do anything of that nature, are you?"

"From the looks of this place, none of that would help me. Where the hell can I run to?" Paulie laughed and shook his head at the same time.

"You're funny and very observant. That's good. It'll take you places money can't." He opened the door on his side and stepped out, his hand reaching out after for her to follow.

"I can help myself out." She gripped the straps on her backpack and slid out of the limo, her feet hitting the gray coble stone driveway. Her eyes widened at the plentiful oak trees around her that soared towards the heavens, the grass was just as green and full as the other lawns she saw and the house was the biggest house she'd ever seen in her life.

"You-you live here?" She looked over at Paulie before returning to gaze at her new surroundings.

"Yes...and so do you." Nala's gaze suddenly became sad as she replayed the moment she was ripped from her mother's tearful hug. But the feeling of her mother slipping the money KJ had given her from her fingers angered her more, causing her fist to clench her black straps harder. Paulie patted her shoulder and she wiped a small frustrated tear that decided to surface. "Come on. Let me show you around. You won't need this." Paulie removed her

book bag from her and whistled at a nearby worker for him to take it. "If you need anything, ask any of my people around and they will help you." She nodded her head as they walked towards magnificent house.

"This place is huge. I think it's bigger than the Prescott Mall." Nala took a sip from a water bottle Paulie had given her during the tour of the kitchen.

"Counting the land? Way bigger." He laughed as the continued down a hallway decorated with paintings and statues. "Believe it or not, I didn't come from money. I lived in a place worse than your old apartment."

"What's worse than my old apartment?"

"Ever sleep in a homeless shelter or on the streets?"

"No...have you?"

"A few times."

"Oh...sorry..." Nala lowered her head.

"Do not be sorry for something you didn't know anything about." Paulie lifted her chin. "Instead, be understanding and humbled. Princesses and future queens do not cower."

"Yea well, I ain't no princess."

"Oh, but you are. You just haven't discovered her yet." Paulie stopped at a door. "I suppose you know what this room is."

"Well you showed me everything except where I sleep." Nala shrugged her shoulders. Paulie turned the knob and pushed the door open and she stepped inside what was her room. Stunned and frozen in her spot, she took in the sights of a brand new and what looked to be fluffy cloud soft bed, a flat screen TV that hung on the wall opposite of the bed with a vanity mirror and table below it. She took small steps inside, looking at every shiny new thing in the room that was now hers.

"There are some clothes in your closet and dresser. I'll take you to get more things tomorrow, but I had my shopper pick out a few things to see if we can get an idea of what you like." Paulie stepped inside the room taking notice of her silent and unmoving disposition. "And sorry your walls aren't painted yet either, but my assistant Leslie assured me that pink wasn't the right color for a fourteen-year-old girl so..." he laughed nervously. Nala turned to him with a wet face. "We can change whatever you don't like Nala, it's not a problem."

"Why?"

"Why what?"

"Why are you doing this?" she raised her voice. Not because she was angry but because she was truly confused. "Why am I here and why can't mom be here with me?"

"I would love to give you those answers and I will," Paulie sighed and walked towards her, "just not today." Nala rolled her eyes and scoffed. "But I promise you that I will one day. Don't worry about those things right now. Continue to explore. Take a swim. Relax. Do whatever you'd like Nala, this is home. You're home." Nala couldn't hold back her tears so hid her face in her hands and turned from him, shoulders shuddering from her sobs. Paulie turned her back around and gave a warm embrace that softened her cries. "I never experienced the joys of having my own baby girl and my son hasn't cried to me since he was ten, so, forgive me if I'm not the best at this." He continued to hug her for some minutes before his cellphone rang. With one arm he reached into his pocket and took it out. She looked up at him and read his face. The call must be important. "I don't have to answer if you still need me."

"No," she let go of him and wiped her face dry, "I'm fine."

"Okay and remember if you need anything ask around or stop in my office. You remember where it is?" She nodded her head as his phone continued to ring. "Okay I will see you in a few hours for dinner." Paulie walked towards her door.

"Paulie." she called out to him before he could shut it.

"Yes sweetie?" he peeked his head inside.

"...thank you." He smiled and shut the door behind him.

"Damn I wish somebody woulda came and scooped me up like that." Cole laughed as he continued to clear the table and Nala started the dish water. "So Paulie was a good dude for the most part huh?"

"With me he was always good. You might think I'm crazy for saying this, but I miss him. He loved me and protected me and when he went away...so did the love." Cole stood next to her as she began to wash their plates. "I was always protected but loved?" She shook her head, " Dante and I have different views on that." She looked over at his focused face. "You ever been in love?"

"You always wanna talk about me." He laughed.

"Because you're interesting." She smiled and he softened at her compliment.

"I'm aight. And no, I've never been in love. But let's be real, who could love a guy like me anyway?" Cole raised his hands in the air. "Broke and runnin' from the law. Two things I'm sure no sane woman would put up with." He took a small hand towel off the counter and dried whatever dishes washed.

"Women have loved worse, trust me. There are men with crazy amounts of money and wouldn't know how to genuinely love, even if someone threaten to take all their fortune. Some men of the law or even men that spend the day preachin' to others about how they need to do right, go home and hit their wives or children. Love ain't about your status but your heart...Paulie taught me that." Nala looked over at Cole whose eyes were fixed on her. "What?" she shifted her feet nervously.

"Dante's such a fool." Cole shook his head as set the towel down on the counter and headed to the bathroom to start his shower. Cole shut the bathroom door behind him and slid his shirt off over his head. He viewed himself in the mirror at his

107

wildly growing hair, taking a few moments to decipher if he should keep it that way or trim it. For now, he decided to keep it the same. Cole stepped inside the shower and let the water hit his face and chest. *I'm Gloria.* Her face resurfaced in his head. She hadn't really left his mind since their encounter. The way she took interest in him. It didn't feel genuine. And everything Jonathan told him only fueled his feelings of suspicion and uneasiness. He knew that if he didn't keep a watchful eye out, she could become a very big problem.

13.

No Love

Silence covered the room. Their thoughts hey both laid quietly on their backs, staring up at the dark ceiling as they tried not to think about their individual problems. Nala reached for her phone and reread the message she received earlier, tossing it around in her head, trying to decipher the real meaning behind his kind words. *Dante has never in his natural born life talked to me like that. Soudin' all caring and genuine? No way that was him...* Nala put her phone down and glided her fingers across her black gun that she kept beside her each night. Cole tried not to sigh too loud, irritated he wasn't able to shake the events of his day from his mind. *Can't believe this shit... been on the run too long for this to start happening now.* He looked over to Nala. *She don't deserve to be dragged into this shit if I get caught. But I ain't bettin' on that happenin'. Not now, not ever.* He looked back up to the ceiling. A light flashed into the bedroom from the window, startling Nala and Cole. Cole grabbed his gold covered gun that was resting beside the bed and stood up, quietly making his way to the window. Nala picked up her gun and held it firmly by her side as Cole peeked through the blinds to find the source of the light but it was gone. He let out air and relaxed his tense shoulders, Nala doing the same.

"You good?" He asked as he turned on the small lamp got back onto the bed, gun still in his clutch.

"Yea...you?" He looked down at her gun, completely forgetting that she had one.

"I'm straight. You even know how to use that thing?"

"Wanna find out?" she smirked pointing it to him.

"Yea aight." He laughed.

"Paulie got me this gun for my sixteenth birthday. Being the kind of man he was at the time, he wanted to make sure I could protect myself when he or anyone else wasn't around."

"Ever have to use it?" He raised his brow getting back onto the bed.

"Other than target practice no. Dante hid it from me for a while, probably thought I'd shoot him with it one day." She laughed. *Doesn't sound like a bad idea though...*

"I haven't used mine in a while so don't feel too bad." They both returned to their backs and stared up at the ceiling again, only silence and few inches between them.

"I can't believe you've never been in love." Nala turned on her side to face Cole and he shook his head.

"Here you go. What's so hard to believe about it?"

"You're not ugly." Cole laughed. "I mean maybe we need to do something with this hair, but you look good." She patted the top of his growing bush. "Smart. Any person that can run from the law for two years without getting caught is borderline

110

genius. You got some hardware in the toolbox." Nala winked and Cole laughed hard.

"Shut up."

"AND underneath that hard ass exterior you-"

"Don't call me soft cause I ain't."

"I was going to say likable." She rolled her eyes. "Really, I like talking to you. Feels like I'm lookin' in the mirror sometimes."

"I'm aight but your reflection is the one I wouldn't mind starin' at all the time." Nala's cheeks burned from smiling so hard.

"And you say things like that. There has to be a girl somewhere out there who's crazy about you."

"I thought so too but I think she just loved what could do for her."

"Those are the worst kind of females, trust me, I know a few." Nala shook her head.

"Me and love ain't never been friends anyway. I learned that a long time ago. It ain't enough to get you what you want."

"Well what is?"

"I don't know." Cole rubbed his beard.

"Well I guess the better question is what do you want?"

"If I could buy my freedom I would but I might as well forget that. My own house again, my own whip. And money. Same shit everyone wants." He looked over at her quiet face. "What's wrong?"

"Just thinking about that house of endless rooms, different cars for everyday of the week and money I could spend for hours without even scratch the surface of my account...and how it's not enough. Don't get me wrong all that is nice, but those things were never able to fill the empty spaces in my heart." Nala fell into his gaze of curiosity. "I think love is enough. Cause that house can crumble, the cars can rust, and the money could burn. But the love a mother or father, friend or even a stranger, it's gotta be the greatest thing to have." She smiled and Cole could help but smile as well. "You must think I'm crazy."

"Nah." Cole turned to her, their noses barely missing each other. "You're perfect." The pounding in Cole's heart quickened the longer he continued to examine her. *I know if I kiss you, it's just gonna make things worse.*

Kiss me. Nala gave him a soft smile.

Fuck it. Before their lips could touch, sounds of glass being smashed startled and separated them. Swiftly Cole grabbed ahold of his gun again. The smashing became louder and shrieking laughter joined in sounding as if they were right outside the house. Nala grabbed her gun and got up off the bed as Cole moved towards the bedroom door.

"What you think you doin?" Cole whispered to him as she came up behind him.

"I'm gonna cover you." She whispered back.

"Shit if you are! You don't know what's out there."

"And you don't either so I'm goin' with you." Cole didn't object as the smashing continued. Cole cocked his gun and opened the bedroom door, Nala following suit. The living room was dark and empty, just as they'd left it, so he moved to the front door and opened it without hesitation. Not too far down on his sidewalk was a group of junkies smashing some old pipes and liquor bottles. Cole lowered his gun to his side and shook his head.

"Heeeyy it's the mean man!" Brittany smashed a forty-ounce bottle and her insanely high friends rejoiced. "Wanna come hang with us?"

"Ayo how many times I gotta ask y'all to keep that shit down the street? You know what time it is?"

"It's time for another hit! Jamal," she sang, "get the shit ready. Come on mean man just take one hit. And where's that princess at? Where she live at? Go find princess out here so she can party with us too. I told Jamal how pretty she is, she looks just like-"

"Take y'all asses on away from my house with that shit before I start makin' some real noise out here." Cole flashed them his gun.

"Told y'all, this nigga is crazy." A tall and overly skinny man with a few needles and pipes in his hands backed away from the curb and started down the street, the group of fiends following the thin man holding their poison.

"Aww damn mean man, you scared away all my friends."

"They're smart, you might wanna follow 'em." Cole pointed down the street with his gun.

113

"Okay but before I do, let me hold somethin'." She started to walk closer to him but once more he pointed his gun and this time, she scurried off in the direction her group went. Cole looked back inside the house to see Nala by the front door with a look of worry on her face.

"Guess I don't have to ask who "Princess" is." He stepped back inside and shut the door behind him. "I thought I told you not to talk to anyone. Now that fiend ass bitch knows we know each other."

"Okay it's not like I willingly started a conversation with her. As far as she knows, I don't even know you." Nala rolled her eyes and went back inside the bedroom.

"Don't let her bein' a crack head fool you. I've seen her get a few niggas caught up around here so she's capable of anything."

"Okay Cole."

"You never who she's runnin' her mouth to and how far that word might travel." Cole went on as Nala sat in the middle of the bed. "And don't think any of the rest of those motherfuckers out there are any different."

"I said okay Cole. Damn." She sighed and sat against the wall. Cole sighed as well and joined her, placing his hand on her thigh.

"I don't mean to be hard but I'm serious. We gotta watch our backs. We can't do anything that'll draw attention to us."

"You're right." She placed her hand on top of Cole's. "I have to be more careful."

Vanessa yawned as she filled up her cup with coffee for the fourth time. Her eyes were screaming for darkness and her body just wanted to rest but all she chose to think about was Anderson. He was single with no children and handsome, just like Cole. Though the bag boy provided little information, his attitude towards her gave her the feeling she was right about her attractive mark. She returned to her chair at the computer that was playing back the footage from the store's parking lot cameras and scanned the numerous pages of entrance and departure times she wrote down along with the car types and colors to try and pin Anderson's vehicle.

"It's like the guy is a fuckin' magician." She slammed her pen down onto her legal pad, frustrated that she still had nothing. "He outta teach a class." She leaned back in her chair, kicking her feet up and taking a drink from her coffee. She quietly stared at the screen for some minutes before sitting her cup down on her desk and placing her feet on the floor. She went back a few pages on her legal pad with a raised brow. "That's weird." She scrolled back the footage and intently stared at the screen. "A black sedan exited the parking lot at five fifty-three..." she went back a few pages, "But I don't have an entrance time for it." Excitement over came her as she scrolled back the video back a few times just to verify. "Gimme a face or a license plate, that's all I need." She paused on the frame of the vehicle exiting the parking lot and zoomed in on it. "Only half the plate, of course..." Vanessa shook her head but a spark of hope ignited a satisfied smile on to her face. "But I'll take it."

14.

The Things You Do, Effect Me Too...

Nala laid at one end of the couch and flipped through channels to find something entertaining as Cole sat the other end writing for his usual thirty minutes. His fingers found her legs to be their own personal playground, exploring and roaming their smooth surface, her feet resting comfortably in his lap. A slight smile brushed across his face and he chuckled as his other hand glided across the paper. Nala raised her brow.

What's so funny?"

"Nothin' nosy." She moved closer to him to take a peek at what he was writing. "Uh, whatchu think you doin'?" He shielded his book.

"I just wanna take a look since you won't tell me." She reached for the book, but he held it out of her reach.

"Cause, it's not meant for you look or know what's in it then huh?" She grabbed for the book again but no success.

"Let me see." She climbed over him but a strong hand he held her back her advances. "Fine." Nala got up from the couch, went into the kitchen and opened up the fridge, scanning for food. She grabbed some leftover pasta and shut the door. "Tough question but what do you do for fun around here? I know you're limited but still there has to be somethin'."

117

"I'm sure my definition and your definition of fun are different. Fun for me is kickin' back, havin' a beer or five while watchin' the game." He joined her in the kitchen, leaning up against one of the counters.

"Well I like being outside."

"Clearly." Cole laughed and Nala rolled her eyes as she placed the pasta in the tiny microwave next to him.

"I just wanna do somethin' that doesn't involve being confined inside four walls. I'm almost jealous of Brittany and her crack crew. They sound like they be havin' a ball outside."

"Yea but you know why."

"I know, I'm just looking for any excuse to be outside." Cole stared at her sulking face as she watched the pasta filled bowl rotate in the microwave.

"There's a park about a mile from here. If you don't mind walking, I'll take you." He draped him arm over her shoulder and she smiled widely up at him.

"Foreal?"

"I can tell you itchin' to be outside. I'on wantchu walkin' round here with ya lip poked out either so yea, I'll take you when I come back."

"Come back?" Nala's eyebrows furrowed to the middle of her forehead as she removed the pasta from the heated pasta from the microwave.

"Yea I have some business to handle for a couple days."

"When were you going to tell me?" Nala took a seat at the small round table in the kitchen, attitude dripping from her voice. Cole took a seat next to her. "Or was I gonna wake up to you being gone?"

"I honestly forgot to tell you Nala."

"And like usual, I'm just supposed to sit here and do nothing. Maybe I should go hang out with Brittany? She's practically been beggin' for my company." She sarcastically threw out.

"That's not even funny Nala." Cole's face hardened. "You can go hang out with Bashi. You know he doesn't mind havin' you there."

"I don't need another person keepin' secrets and lyin' to me." Losing the desire to fill her belly, Nala pushed the bowl away from her and got up from the table.

"And what does that mean?" Cole got up from the table.

"You lie to me, Bashi lied to me. What the hell is with the secrecy?"

"What's Bashi got to do with this? There ain't no secrets. There's just some shit you don't need to know." Nala rolled her eyes and brushed past him to the bedroom, him hot on her heels.

"Why?" She glared over at him as she began to gather her things to shower. "We can talk about our crackhead mamas, Dante and you runnin' from the law but this "business"? All of a sudden there's

119

things I don't need to know. That's bullshit Cole and you know it." Cole stood silent. He was trying not to allow anger to flood his system but the more Nala went in on him, the hotter he became. He had to go. Nala stopped in the middle of her rant once she noticed Cole gathering his hoodie, gun and shoes. "Where are you goin?"

"I need to step out for some air cause you trippin'." He spoke in a low calm tone, slipping his shoes on.

"So, you just gonna walk out?" He ignored her, placing his hoodie over his head and tucking the gun in its front pouch. "Cole-"

"You know what?" Cole stood before her, "I've been fine on my own without you. I wasn't answerin' to nobody before and I ain't startin' that shit now just cause you're here. If you don't like it," he nodded towards the front door, "there's your fuckin' exit." He threw his hood over his head and exited the bedroom, slamming the front door hard behind him. Cole let out a long breath as soon as he made it outside and started towards Bashi's restaurant.

"Heeeyyy there mean man." Brittany called out to him from her usual post on the broken steps of the abandoned green house not far from Bashi's restaurant. "Damn, yous especially mean tonight. What's wrong? Mad the Princess doesn't want you?" She laughed and slapped her knee. "Prissy bitches like her don't want guys like you anyway. They want guys with cars and money. You? You ain't got none of that shit." She laughed harder.

"You seem real interested in her." Cole slowed his walking pace.

"Aren't we all?"

"You know anything about her?"

"Maybe," Brittany sniffed, "but you should know I'm not cheap." Brittany sang and snapped her fingers.

"Just tell me what you know, and I'll take care of you." Brittany peered at him and sucked her teeth.

"I guess. Well mean man, I on't know much. 'Cept for the fact that she ain't from round here. She prolly ain't got no money either, not the way she dresses. But she's so pretty. Haven't you seen her?"

"Once or twice walkin."

"Ugh she's so pretty. Jamal really digs her."

"She ever hang out with y'all?"

"Hmph, please. I invited her to a couple parties but like you and that fat black man, she don't want no parts. So strange! Who doesn't like a good party? Maybe one day I'll find her house and throw her a surprise party."

"Mm, good luck with that."

"Hey hey! What about my payment?" Brittany held out her hand. Cole sucked his teeth and reached down in his pockets for a twenty and handed it to her.

"Don't ever say I ain't let you hold nothin'."

"Aww thanks mean man! Wait til I tell Jamal!" She jumped down from the steps and ran off in the opposite direction Cole was going. Cole shook his head and strolled the rest of the way to Bashi's. He was happy Nala told him the truth about not giving any info to Brittany and started to question why it was hard for him to do the same. The bell sounded when he opened the door.

"Well I wasn't expectin' to see you here."

"Yea me either honestly." Cole flopped down into one of the chairs and Bashi came from behind the counter with two cold brews in his hands.

"Oh shucks, that's the look of a man with some woman troubles." Bashi set the beer in front of Cole and Cole took a long drink.

"Women... Such nosy, emotional beautiful creatures. At least this one is..."

"I take it the little lady is becoming antsy about your "job"."

"Figured she already poked around the subject with you."

"I didn't want to be the one to tell her. She's an observant girl, she's going to figure it out on her own Cole whether you tell her or not." Bashi could see that Cole was almost done with his brew so he went behind the counter to grab a few more.

"I almost want her to figure it out, that way I don't have to tell her." Cole stared down at his cold half empty bottle.

"You afraid she'll look at you differently?" Bashi returned with more cold beers and the wooden box he kept his Dominos in.

"Kinda."

"No offense kid but you can't get any worse." They both chuckled. "I'm sure she knows whatever you're doin' ain't right and I doubt she'll like you any less because of it."

"I doubt it. Not after what I just said." Cole moved the beers out the way and Bashi spilled the dominoes onto the table and shuffled them.

"Well what'd you say?"

"Told her I was fine before she got here and I ain't about to start answerin' to nobody."

"That don't sound too bad." Bashi took his seven tiles from the pile.

"Mmm… I told her if she ain't like it, she knows where the exit is." Cole gathered his seven tiles.

"Knowing you, it probably didn't come out as nice as you just said." Bashi chuckled and sipped from his beer.

"I messed up, didn't I?"

"Nahhhh, just said somethin' you didn't mean. I'm sure you both said some things to each other that wasn't necessary. Y'all just pushin' each other's button." Bashi began their game by slapping down a domino.

"I should prolly go apologize." Cole took his turn.

"Yes but give yourselves some time. She'll be there when you get back."

"Aye man I swear you cheat." Cole laughed as he and Bashi exited the restaurant, Bashi locking the doors behind himself. "Can't wait for the day I beat you."

"Well young man you'll be waitin' a long time cause I'm the king of dominos. Those are my lucky dominos too. Never lost a game with those bad boys."

"One of these days man." They both laughed. "Thanks Bashi for helpin' me get away and talkin' to me. I really appreciate it..."

"You know I'm here anytime. You gonna be okay walkin' home?"

"Of course." Cole patted the front of his hoodie pocket. "You want me to walk you home?"

"You know I'm fine." Bashi touched his own jacket pocket. "Go home and be nice. And honest."

"Yea if she's still there." Cole threw over his shoulder as he proceeded on with his walk. Cole walked the oddly quiet street, Brittany nor her crew anywhere to be found. "That twenty must go a long way." Cole stomach dropped a bit when he approached his home and saw the lights out. He opened the front door and was met with pure silence and darkness. He closed and locked the front door behind him, stumbling a bit as he made his way to the bedroom. Quietly, he opened the door and let out a silent breath at the sight of her curled up under the covers. He took his gun out his hoodie pocket and set it on the dresser before removing the hoodie from his chest. Nala peeked through her eye lids to see a shirtless Cole removing

124

his shoes trying not to make any noise. She shut her eyes tight once Cole took his gun from off the dresser and made his way to his side of the bed. He got under the covers and laid on his back, staring up at the ceiling. *Thank you, Lord, for another day. Thank you for Nana. I pray she keeps livin' healthy and safe like she's been doin'. Please watch over me when I do this job tomorrow... Amen.* Cole finished his prayer and looked over at Nala's back. Nala stared at the wall in front of her, feeling his eyes on her. *Maybe I should wake her up and talk.... Nah, leave her alone. I ain't tryna start another argument.* Nala felt his arm slip under the covers and pull her close to his bare chest. She could smell the beer on his breath, but she didn't care. His touch was warm. His hold was strong and comforting. Nala basked in his embrace and drifted off to sleep but Cole laid awake as he held Nala. *And God...about Nala...* he began to pray again.

Cole was awakened by the beeping on his watch and he automatically dreaded getting up for the day. He silenced it and opened his eyes to find a sleeping Nala still in his grasp, her hand resting lightly on top of the arm he had wrapped around her. The sun was barely above the horizon, so he decided to take five more minutes to enjoy her warmness against his. She turned over, allowing Cole to take in her peace filled face as she rested her hand on his chest. His strong pounding heart under her fingertips brought her to life, her eyes happy his face was the first thing they saw.

"I shouldn't have blown up at you like that."

"I deserved it. I shoulda told you sooner...and about my job-"

"I don't have to know every single detail about whatever you do. I just don't want you to lie to me." She looked up at him as he rubbed her shoulder while staring up at the ceiling. He contemplated on telling her but again, he thought the timing was wrong. So he settled for telling her when he returned.

"I won't if you don't." He looked down into her sparkling brown eyes.

"You got it." Their gaze on each other was a long and sweet as his hand continued to rub her, those familiar goose bumps returning to her skin. The strong pounding under her hand was replaced with light thumping. He moved closer to her lips but quickly groaned and pulled away.

"As much as I want to, I'm not kissing you with morning breath." They both laughed as she sat up and blushed as he got up off the mattress. She watched him with admiration while he gathered his things to shower and head out the bedroom door.

"So how long will you be gone?" she followed him into the bathroom. He turned on the shower head and set the water temperature to his liking.

"Just a couple of days." Without warning, his sweats and boxers fell to the floor and he stepped into the shower, Nala getting a peek of course. " Whatchu gonna do when I'm gone?" Cole poked his head from behind the shower curtain.

126

"Oh, I don't know," she fluffed her hair up in the mirror, "probably just hang out with Bashi. Wish I had book to read or somethin'." That was one of the perks of living in a grand house such as Paulie's. There was always something to do. "You want somethin' to eat before you go?"

"Nah, I'll grab somethin' on the way." Cole went on with his shower and Nala returned to the room. When he came back into the room fully clothed, she was lying in bed playing a game on her phone as usual. Her stomach sunk a little at the sight of him putting his shoes on a feeling of slight sadness overcoming her, but she wasn't gonna let him see it. He stood to his feet with his hoodie in hand and gun tucked in the waist band of his jeans.

"Bout ready?" Nala stood up as he pulled his hoodie over his head.

"Yup." He pulled her into a tight warm hug. She took in his fresh shower scent. "You know you have my number if you need me but try not to call. Text me if anything."

"Okay." He stared down into her face and that urge crept back inside him. Her eyes shimmered as if they were begging him to do it.

"I hate goodbye kisses..." He confessed, a flash back of his mom landing a sweet kiss on him before she turned him away to him grandmother.

"But you're coming back...right?" She raised her brow at him. He laughed to himself. She was too smart, and he loved it. Bravely, Cole leaned down and kissed her lips as softly as he knew how.

"I'll be back."

Dante sat up in bed as he watched the morning news and waited for one of his girls to bring him up breakfast. Though he had the company of Jade and Natalia the night before, he'd had a horrible night's sleep due Nala and his father invading his usually carefree mind. Angrily he snatched his phone off the nightstand to see if Nala had responded to the sincere and concerned text he had Big Joey conjure up, hoping it would break her down and force her to get in contact with him. His blood burned within him as he met the blank screen of his phone, causing him to slam the phone back onto the dresser.

"Good morning Dante." Sasha, his newest girl entered the majestic room Dante and Nala shared together. The walls were cream colored to match their cream and real gold speckled marble canopy bed. The king size bed was covered in the softest thousand thread count Egyptian cotton sheets that felt as if one were sleeping in a field of feathers. There were two grand windows high and wide, allowing one to overlook the entire back yard that contained a large pool, tennis court, basketball court and walking garden that was decorated with a myriad of wildflowers.

"Good morning." He dryly returned. She kept her best smile on as she brought over his pancakes smothered in butter and syrup with bacon and eggs as well as freshly squeezed orange juice. All prepared by her.

"I hope you're hungry." She sang placing the tray over his lap. She placed a kiss on his cheek. "Your morning paper as well. How are you?" she took a seat on the side of the bed, anxious to see if he'd compliment her cooking skills.

"Fine." He shoved a bacon slice into his mouth before cutting into his pancakes.

"If I may say so Dante, you seem a little down. Ever since that one girl Nala left-"

"I don't need anything else from you. You're dismissed." He spoke not even bothering to look up at her. She sat there for a few more seconds before quietly exiting to room. A heavy knock sounded on his door not too long after. "Come in."

"What'd you do to that poor girl? She's crying her little eyes out." Big Joey entered the room alone and shut the door behind him.

"Don't know and honestly don't care. Got any news for me?"

"No sir. Checked every shelter and hotel within the area and she hasn't been to any of them. I even checked online to see if there were any boarding house's she might've ducked into but nothing." Dante laughed as he removed the tray from his lap and got out of bed.

"I knew I should've put a tracker on her fuckin' phone after the last time she thought she could get out of here." Dante smoothly walked to his side of the closet and began to pick out his outfit for the

129

day. He paused for a moment as he stood about his dress shirts. "I wonder if my connect down at the precinct can get ahold of her phone records, see if she's made any calls or if any calls have been made to her." Big Joey shook his head.

"With everything coming up, I don't think it's best for you to draw any type of legal attention to yourself."

"You're right but I have to get a handle on this before it's out of my control. somethin' I can control." Dante pulled out a blood red shirt and laid it on the island that sat in the middle of the closet and thought for a moment as he stared down at the deep intense color. "...what if I sent one of the girls?" He looked over at Joey with a sly grin.

"It could possibly work." Big Joey confirmed. Dante clapped his hands and laughed loudly at what he thought was a brilliant idea.

"Tell Sasha to come here then."

"Sasha?" Big Joey questioned. "Why her? She's new, she's also the youngest and she doesn't know how we operate around here. It's best if you use one of the others, like Jade." Big Joey tried to sway him.

"You just gave me every reason to use Sasha. Young and naïve means she's easier to mold into whatever I please. So, as I said, go get her Joey." Big Joey said nothing more and left out as Dante stripped down to his naked body and waited. Sasha knocked lightly at the door and was beyond surprised and excited to see a bare Dante answer. "Come in here baby." He took her by the hand and shut the door. "I want

130

to apologize for how I spoke to you earlier. I didn't mean to be an asshole. I just been under a lot stress lately." He raised her shirt above her head and traced his fingers over the top of her breasts.

"It's okay Dante." She bit her lip as she rubbed his chest. "I don't want be stress in your life."

"No, it's not okay. I don't like when my girls cry, especially when I'm the reason." He kissed her lips and she immediately wiped the memory of their encounter from her brain. This was a moment for her and Dante to really connect and she wasn't about to waste the moment by sulking.

"I'm sure you can think of a way to make it up to me and relieve your stress at the same time."

"You're right." He led her to the bed she'd been waiting to sleep in. Bend over."

15.

While You Were Away

A naked Sasha smiled to herself as she continued to roll a blunt while Dante showered and dressed for the day's events. She crawled to the edge of the bed and lit up, Dante finally returning from the closet dressed in the red button up he picked out before he summoned her. *Mmm…this man of mine…* Sasha watched him decorate his wrist with a platinum and diamond watch, her admiration and desire for him growing stronger by the minute. They finally caught eyes. He grinned at her sweet young face before placing a kiss on her forehead.

"You doin' alright?" He asked.

"Couldn't be better." She blew out smoke and passed him the blunt, "You have a busy day today?"

"Just showing my face a few places and then I'll be back."

"There anything I can do while you're gone?" Dante inhaled once more before passing the blunt back to her. *Never been asked that before.*

"For now, no. How about you go have a spa day, on me." He kissed her lips and she smiled hard on the inside. "I want you glowing when I return home." He slid on his suit jacket, finally ready to meet Big Joey downstairs. "And buy something I can rip off later."

"You got it." She placed the blunt between her lips and stood to her feet to straighten Dante's black tie on him. "Perfect."

"Thank you, baby girl. Alright, I'm out."

"Be safe." She called out to him before he shut the bedroom door behind him. Sasha took a long pull and exhaled both smoke and satisfaction as she looked about the majestic room. Leaving the gold specked bed, she opened one of two ten-foot-tall French doors and stepped on to the sun lit balcony. a cool breeze soothed her skin. She loved the sound of the birds tweeting loudly around her. It made her feel as if they were welcoming her home. "Who would give this up?" Sasha continued to smoke as she strolled back inside to the closet. She ran her finger over Nala's fine gowns and casual clothing and shook her head in awe at her collection of stilettos on shelves above her. "She's gotta be fuckin' crazy to run away from all this." Her hand stopped on Nala's silk white robe ad Sasha instantly fell in love. She slipped it on to her shoulders, the soft fabric tickling her skin along the way. Over to Dante's side she went to explore his collection of black suits and different colored dress shirts he owned. She adored his style of dark clothing and shiny ornate jewelry pieces. She picked up his gold and diamond encrusted Cuban link chain and placed it over her head, the heavy and expensive item resting neatly in the midst of her flawless breast. Sasha entered the grand bathroom where she met a jacuzzi tub sat in the midst of the room, a large walk-in glass rain shower behind it. A floor length mirror was to the left and his and her cream marble vanity sinks with gold faucet accents to the right.

Sasha stared at herself in the floor length mirror, falling in love with the way the robe and chain complimented her chocolate skin. The place was absolutely fit for a king and queen and now that the head queen was gone, Sasha decided it was time she fill her spot. "I'm not giving this up."

"I was startin' to think you was gon' punk out on me." Don pulled from the blunt that was keeping his fingers company as Cole sat comfortably in the passenger's side of Don's gold sedan.

"Nah, I don't punk out when It comes to money." Cole peeked into his sideview mirror.

"I feel it." Don tried to pass his stick of green gold over to Cole, but he declined like usual. "I don't get how you don't smoke man."

"I don't need that shit in my system if I get caught up."

"Shit. You don't smoke, don't drink the good shit or get no pussy. Glad I ain't duckin from the law. Not drinkin' is cool but pussy and weed? Can't live without it." Cole shook his head as he looked out the window and wished he were back at the house chillin' with Nala instead of listening to Don's nonsense. "So, tell me changed your mind about Bailey Estates?" Don looked over at Cole.

"It's too high risk."

"Shit nigga you need to take a risk with yo square ass."

"One: have you seen Bailey Estates? The floor levels in those homes are too big for the two of us to sweep quickly. And two: we have to go through an armed security officer just to get in to damn the community."

"But you forgot number three: we gon' get paid. And not just the lil money we been makin'. As far as the security officer and floor levels go, that's why we need the third person. If we could find a bitch who has finesse like us, we'd be straight.

"A bitch?" Cole raised his eyebrow.

"Yea," Don inhaled, "If shawty look good and know how to work what she got, we could get past the guard at the gate. I'm tellin' you it'd be easy money." The smoke poured from his lips. "And maybe you could finally get you some pussy." Don chuckled as he put out his blunt and leaned his seat back.

"Whose spot is this anyway?" Cole changed the subject. Don handed Cole a magazine with a middle-aged black man on the front of it. He was dressed in a navy-blue suit and silver bowtie and silver cuff links to match. He made sure his pinky was up to show off the diamond encrusted band that settled on it. His head was bald and shiny, and his smile looked like a million bucks. "Lester Givens?" Cole flipped through the magazine. "This nigga is loaded. I know he ain't confine himself to a loft."

"Oh yea, he's loaded alright. This is ONE of his places. Gotta say I was pretty proud of myself when I came across it."

"And how you do that?"

"Don't worry bout it. Just know this is solid."

"I don't believe he lives here...all that money?" Cole looked out at the lofts. They weren't as flashy and luxurious like Lester's many beach houses and mansions.

"Yea well when you tryna hide your side bitch from your wife, you might not wanna splurge on fancy new houses. I'm sure he givin' his wife an all-black card just to keep her happy. Give just about any female some money and some dick, she'll do just about anything. That includes ignore her nigga fuckin' and trickin' off on other women." Cole shook his head and leaned his seat back.

"Both are stupid if you ask me. "

"Hmph, if you had his money, what would you do?"

"Not what he's doin', that's for damn sure. Been there, done that." Don shrugged his shoulders and went back to looking out to the lofts.

"This place is sketchy as fuck." Vanessa spoke into her cellphone as stepped out her car onto the cracked concrete and looked around at the rundown neighborhood. "It doesn't even look like anyone lives here. Maybe that address was bogus." She made sure her car door was locked as well as her gun in her waist band.

"It used to thrive with people and business back in the early seventies but once the drugs hit, everybody either moved, died from the drugs or

137

went to jail. It's pretty much an abandoned neighborhood now." Her co-worker Dave explained to her.

"It's not that abandoned." Vanessa took note of the group of loud junkies across the street who were dancing and laughing with each other.

"You need some backup?"

"No, I'm fine. I can handle crack heads. I'm gonna take a look around, try and find this place. I'll call you once I'm done." She hung up and ran her hand across her gun once more, just for comfort. She looked to her left and saw more abandoned houses, to the right there was what looked like a small corner store and more housing. To the corner store she proceeded, the group of junkies getting louder as she passed by them.

"Hey baby, you wanna party with us?" A tall and very skinny man called out to her.

"Shut the hell up Jamal! I'm gettin' tired of havin to share!" A woman in a holey green shirt and ripped jeans shoved his shoulder. Faster Vanessa's feet carried her to the corner store. The bell sounded as she pushed the heavy door open, a cool breeze of air greeting her.

"Hi there." The older gentleman at the counter smiled at her.

"Hi." she returned. "How are you today?"

"I can't complain, can I get you somethin' to eat?"

"This is a restaurant?" she peeked over at the grill.

"I call it a multi-purpose eatery sometimes." The man chuckled and his shoulders bounced. "I cook food and sell things people passing through might need." Vanessa nodded her head as she continued to look around. "My name is Bashi by the way."

"Detective Vanessa Frazier." She shook his hand and Bashi raised his brow.

"Detective? Ha! I haven't seen one of you in over thirty years. What brings you by this way?"

"I'm looking for someone and I feel like he may have been through here. Have you seen this man?" Vanessa pulled up a picture of Cole on her phone and held it to Bashi's face. He squinted his eyes at the picture and shook his head.

"I've come across a lot of people in my time here but not him. Can't miss someone as light bright as he is."

"He is pretty bright." Vanessa nodded her head and shoved her phone in her back pocket, Bashi catching a glimpse of her gun on her hip. "Your car was spotted on camera exiting the Ruthford shopping center a couple days ago, were you there?"

"Yes...I was." Bashi rubbed his chin. "I ran out of fresh fruit and milk so I made a quick purchase."

"Can you verify that? Have any receipts or anything to prove you were there?"

"I tossed it to the recycling bin outside. I already have enough clutter as it is." He laughed again and she laughed with him.

"You sound like my late grandfather. He hated receipts. Said they were a complete waste and horrible for the environment. If he were alive, I'm sure he'd be a faithful recycler still." She leaned against the counter.

"He sounded like he was a smart man."

"He was very smart. Always stood for what was right. My mother says I'm just like him. " she smiled lightly. "You have any grandchildren?"

"No, but I would've loved the experience."

"I'm sure those characters outside keep you on your toes enough. You outta move."

"Actually," Bashi took a seat on his stool, "they don't bother me much. No one's broken in or vandalized anything of mine so there's really no need to uproot myself."

"Nice to know people like that still have some respect I guess." Vanessa leaned up off the counter and reached in her wallet. "Well if you happen to come across this gentleman or if you just need help in general, take my card and don't hesitate to call me." She held it out to him and he took it from her fingers.

"I highly doubt I will but thank you. If you're looking for someone who might be in hiding, I'd say start your search over in Griffin. A lot of shady characters there. It's about forty-five minutes from here, would you like directions?" Bashi searched for a pen and piece of paper.

"No sir but thank you. That just might be where I need to go. I appreciate the help."

"You're welcome." Bashi called out before she exited the restaurant. Bashi sat back down in his stool. "Shit Cole..." Vanessa decided to get back in her car after her conversation with Bashi. Clearly, no one, outside of him, who was in their right mind occupied the neighborhood and she could have better luck in Griffin like Bashi suggested. The group of strung out bums had disappeared, but one person remained.

"Hey fancy woman." A woman in short shorts and a dirty pink tank top called out to her. "Hey! I know you hear me talkin' to you!" Vanessa turned to the woman with a smug look on her face. "I mean shit, you could say hi back or smile."

"I don't have time to fool around with the likes of you. I'm working."

"Only work that gets done round here is the work that someone's got to get on their back or knees for. That don't look like it's in your job description. Or are you one of those fancy hoes that actually put on nice clothes to suck dick?" She laughed loudly, further annoying an already irritated Vanessa. "Cause, I don't see the point in that. They just gon mess up your clothes anyway."

"No." Vanessa looked the woman up and down. "I'm a detective."

"Oh shit, I was just joking lady honestly." The woman scratched at her skin and stood up.

"Sounded like a confession to prostitution so should I arrest you now or do you think you can help me out with somethin'?"

"I ain't no snitch if that's what you want me to do. Besides, I gotta go find my friends-"

"Oh no you don't." Vanessa stepped closer to her. "Not before you answer a couple questions... what's your name?"

"Brittany." she sniffed. "We done here?"

"Not even close. What kind of drugs are you on?"

"Really bitch?"

"I need to know what kind of junkie I'm dealing with. That way I know if you're just talkin' out your ass or if your information is actually valid so answer the damn question, bitch. What are you on?" Brittany sucked her teeth and scratched her head as she looked around the neighborhood. No one was around.

"Crack. Sometimes heroin but not a lot. That's more of Kiki and Jamal's thing. She prolly got her hands all over him and some goods right now so let me go." She tried to walk past but Vanessa stepped in her way, blocking her path.

"Oh I'm sure she doesn't mind me stealing you for a bit. This guy ever come through here?" She held up the same picture of Cole that she showed Bashi. "He ever buy or sell you any drugs? Pay you for your overused talents?" Brittany stared hard at the picture, immediately recognizing the man in the picture. Vanessa watched Brittany as she gazed at the picture. "You know him, don't you?" She moved the phone closer to Brittany's dancing eyes.

"I don't but I'd DAMN sure like to know him! Who is that fine piece of man? He looks like he a good

142

time. I think I'd give him a fifty percent discount. He yo boyfriend or somethin'?" Vanessa rolled her eyes and shoved her phone back into her back pocket.

"Shoulda known."

"Can I go now?" Brittany whined. Vanessa stepped to the side and let her pass, shaking her head as she watched her disappear down the street. "What a complete waste of time." She turned to walk back to her car but there was a young woman in hoodie and sweatpants walking her way. She didn't look dangerous and from where Vanessa could tell, she didn't look like she was on drugs either. "Hey there."

"Hi?" Nala slowed her stroll.

"You okay?"

"Yea." Nala looked the woman up and down, catching notice of the gun on the woman's waist. "Why?"

"I'm sorry you just...you just look like you don't belong here that's all."

"What makes you say that?"

"You don't look like the rest of those fools around here making noise and doing drugs."

"You'd be surprised." Nala sniffed and looked past Vanessa to Bashi's. "I'm trying to stop usin' so I work at this restaurant, but you know, it's hard sometimes."

"I'm sorry, let me remember my manners, I'm Vanessa." Vanessa smiled and held out her hand.

143

"Princess." Nala took her hand and shook it lightly before letting it go. "I'm gonna be late." Nala sniffed again and walked around Vanessa.

"Wait! I did want to ask you a question." Vanessa pulled out her phone again and brought up Cole's picture. "Any chance you've seen this man?" Nala glanced quickly at the picture then into Vanessa's eyes.

"No." She turned on her heel and as if on que, Brittany was coming back down the street.

"Princessssss!" Brittany shouted and Nala made her way towards her. Vanessa sighed and shook her head.

"Guess she is just like the rest of them." Vanessa crossed the street and got into her car. Nala stopped in front of Brittany and shushed her quietly, waiting for Vanessa's engine to start.

"You okay?" Nala asked Brittany once she heard the engine sound and Vanessa's car pull away.

"Yea. That bitch was pokin' round here, askin' me all types of questions, makin' me nervous." Brittany shook herself. "I had to get away from her."

"What did she ask you?" Nala looked over her shoulder.

"Bout how I get high and what not. Usual cop shit."

"She told you she's a cop?" Nala turned back to Brittany with curiosity.

"I think. Hell she almost tried to arrest me but I'm too smart. She showed me a picture of the mean man in the neighborhood. Do you know him? He's kinda tall with a cool bush and beard. Oh, and light skinned. Can't forget that cute smooth lookin' light skin." Nala cringed inside at the way Brittany was lusting over Cole. "I keep tellin' him bout you. I think you guys would make a cute couple. You'll finally have that prince you been tryna find. That's why you out here right?" Nala laughed.

"I ain't here to find no prince. So, what did you say to her?"

"I told her I ain't know him, even though I do. He good people on the inside. I can tell." Nala smiled and looked over to the restaurant.

"I guess you are too huh?"

"I have my times." Brittany snapped and they both laughed. "Well I'm sure you gotta go do princess things and I guess I could get high again."

"Or not." Nala smiled back.

"Wouldn't know what else to do Princess..." Brittany gave a slight smile and shrugged her shoulders before walking off to find her usual group of friends and Nala entered the restaurant. Bashi smile big, happy to see her shining face.

"Well hey there." He stepped down from the counter and she met him for a warm hug. "You alright?"

"Yea." Nala removed the hoodie from her body and took a seat at one of the tables. "You?" Bashi joined her at the table with a deck of cards and a bowl of mixed fruit, just like she liked.

145

"I am better now."

"Hmm, you got a surprise visit too huh?" She took a few grapes out the bowl as he set up their five-card game of poker.

"Yep."

"It can't be good if she's this close." Nala shook her head as she picked up her cards.

"No but I don't think she'll be back this way anytime soon. But it seems like you and Cole need to discuss some things." Nala's mouth dropped.

"What this? Why me? Besides, she spoke to you first." Nala stuck out her tongue playfully. She looked at her cards and her burst into enough excitement for Bashi to see she must have a good hand for their poker game.

"Relax over there. You never wanna tell on your hand, even if it's bad and especially when it's good."

"Got it." Nala nodded.

"And you're telling him." Bashi grabbed one card.

"Bashi." She groaned and selected one more card. "Winner tells?" Nala raised her brow as she peeked at him over her cards with a smirk.

"Alright." Bashi laughed in agreement. "Ready?" They both played their cards on the table. "My flush beats your three of a kind Ms. Nala." Nala pouted and Bashi chuckled lightly. "That was a good attempt though. You're learning pretty fast. You actually might beat me." Nala gathered up the cards and shuffled for the next hand.

"Yea but that didn't help me one. Now I have to tell Coke the worst news he's heard in a while I'm sure." Nala's phone vibrated in the pocket of her hoodie and she grabbed it, hoping it was Cole.

"Try not to think about it like that." Bashi took over the cards as she read her screen. Nala excused herself to head to the restroom to use the bathroom. The bathroom door shut behind her as her phone sounded, an unfamiliar number popping up on the phone. She answered the call but did not greet the caller.

"Hello?" Dante's deep voice greeted her. Silence. "Hello?" He called out again, only to still be met with silence. "You realy wanna play this game with me Nala? I'm trying to be nice about this bitch but you're testing my patience and you already know it's been thin with you. I'm giving you three days to get back to the before I really come after you. Trust me, I've got eyes everywhere. And once I catch yo ass I'ma make you wish my father would have just left yo ass where he found you. Three days Nala. Don't make me come lookin' for you." Dante vowed before hanging up.

16.

When I Get Home

"Where are you taking me tonight?" The beautiful woman dressed in a tight red dress with matching heels smiled as she placed a pair of diamond studs in her ears.

"That would spoil the surprise now wouldn't it?" Lester straightened his bowtie in the wide mirror inside of the bathroom. "And we better get a move on." He turned to see the woman checking herself out in the floor length mirror. "I hope you know that dress won't be on for too long tonight." He walked over and kissed her cheek.

"Maybe you can start unwrapping it in the car." She winked at him as she grabbed her white clutch off the dresser.

"Well, let us be on our way then." He took her hand and lead her out of the loft, making sure to lock the door before they proceeded to the elevator. Lester's hand rested the curvaceous woman's hips and he playfully kissed her neck as the doors opened to the ground floor. He held opened the glass door for the lady, Cole off in the shadows of the parking lot, waiting for the signal from Don.

"Good evening Mr. Givens, ma'am." The limo driver greeted the pair and opened the car door for them. The lady slid inside first, Lester following after. The limo pulled off and Cole came out from the darkness.

"They're gone." Cole spoke to Don through his earpiece.

"I'm almost done with this system just give me a second," Don fooled with the security cameras of the building, "still images are in place. Showtime. I'll meet you down there."

"Cool." Cole entered inside the building, hoping he wouldn't run into any of the tenants that occupied the building. He took the exit stairs to the seventh floor where Don was already waiting for him.

"I swear this shit gets easier and easier every time." They slapped hands before Cole took out the tools needed to pick the lock. It didn't take long to hear the click and turn of the lock and they made their way inside. "Shit I knew the top floor had to be the best floor, but this is better than I thought." Don looked about the richly decorated loft. There were a few fine paintings and statues around. "Shit, you think we can lift some of these paintings out of here? I know a guy who always lookin' for artwork like these." Don softly ran his hand over a large scenic gold framed painting.

"We might be able to." Cole took his time as he searched through the living room, not wanting to waste any time. "Let's keep lookin' though."

"You can tell this is side bitch pad." Don shook his head at the pictures of the woman and Lester on the bookcase. "Ain't shit in here."

"Nah, there's somethin' here we can lift. Everything valuable is probably up there." He pointed to the top half of the loft. Don and Cole quietly went up the steps and began to search through the bedroom.

"Money stash." Don held up a handful of stacks of money he found in the underwear drawer that belonged to the woman. "She should've put the money in the bank." Don went back to stuffing some loose jewelry and other items on the dresser and vanity in his bag as Cole made his way into the closet. It wasn't a grand closet, but it was definitely bigger than his current one. Cole knocked on the walls of the closet and touched the base boards for any abnormalities. His fingers came across a small red button on the bottom shelf that Lester kept his expensive dress shoes on.

"There you are." Cole smirked and pressed the button, a secret compartment under the shelf came out and lit up, displaying more money and a brown folder. Cole opened the folder and scanned the documents for valuable information. Most of them were receipts and bank statements regarding purchases he made for his lady friend. "Guess he is smart." Another set of papers detailed of Lester's new owner ship of a security company, as well as a list of residential and commercial properties that used the used to company. Cole took a few snaps before he placed the papers back in their spot and grabbed up the money. Carefully, he closed the compartment and went over onto the woman's side of the closet, figuring she had a couple of items that could fit Nala. She had to be tired of sporting his basketball shorts and sweats with large t-shirts. He took a couple of plain tank tops and three pairs of jeans and shoved them in his bag. He overlooked the closet once more just to make sure he'd gotten everything he wanted and paused. He focused on the light purple object that was hung up on the wall and walked towards it as if he were in a trance. He lifted the silver necklace off its place holder and held it to the light. The round purple amethyst stone sparkled beautifully in the light and Cole smiled, instantly thinking of Nala.

"Yo," Don came into the closet, "find anything?" Cole shoved the necklace in his pocket and turned to Don.

"Yea I got a few things for ya. You ready?"

"Hell yea." Don held up more cash with a sly grin on his face.

"Three days." Continued to echo in Nala's mind as she held her gun and sat quietly in dark bedroom. She'd decided he wouldn't use any f the house lights, not wanting to risk anyone knocking on the door while Cole was away. The gun never felt so heavy in her hands before and she began to wonder it she would have to use it in the coming days. She jumped at the sound of her phone ringing, her snatching it off the bed to see who it was. She smiled and relaxed at the sight of his name.

"Hi." She answered.

"Hey." He returned. "Whatchu doin' up? You're usually knocked out by now." He chuckled and she laughed along with him.

"I guess it's a little different without you here."

"That's nice to know I guess." Cole smiled to himself as Don filled up the tank at the small gas station they stopped at on their way back to town. "How was your day?" She paused for a bit as the whole day's events ran through her head.

"It was fine. Just hung out with Bashi. This phone call must mean that everything on your end is good."

"Yea I'm cool."

"Good." She answered back shortly.

"You okay?"

"Yea...why you ask?"

"I don't know...you're just kinda quiet. You usually have somethin' you wanna talk about." Nala looked around the dark room, the only thing she could see was the blur of the light behind the blinds of the window. There was no noise oddly, just silence.

"Just lonely I guess..."

"I'll be home before you know it. Get some sleep beautiful." Don opened the door to his side of the card and slid inside with a bag of snacks and drinks.

"You be safe." They hung up the phone and Cole reached for a bag of Cheetos.

"Who was that that got you all smilin' and shit over there?" Don quizzed as he pulled away from the gas station.

"No one." Cole looked out the window. Nala put her phone on the charger and got under the covers, moving over to Cole's spot. She never let go of her gun as she closed her eyes and went to sleep.

The next morning, Sasha slowly opened her eyes at the feeling of Dante's hands caressing her thighs and soft kisses against her neck. She placed her hand on his strong chiseled chest.

"Good morning." He kissed her lips and she instantly became wet.

"A good morning it is to wake up next to you." She climbed on top of him and placed many kisses on his chest. "How would you like to start off your morning?"

"That breakfast you made yesterday was bangin'. Natalia uses throws down on the breakfast, but I think I'll put you in charge of that." She smiled hard as he felt on her breast.

"Really?"

"Yea." He nodded, seeing how much his compliment meant to her.

"So, anything in particular you'd like me to make you?"

"Surprise me."

"Okay." Sasha went to climb off him to get started on her task, but he held her hips tight.

"But I need a snack first." Dante leaned up and took one of her nipples into his mouth. She moaned lightly as she slid down onto him. Paige pressed her ear against the door as she listened for Dante's deep voice again but instead heard Sasha's light moans after a few minutes of silence. Paige shook her head as she walked away from the door and made her way down the grand staircase. She entered the kitchen where the Jade and Natalia were dining on their breakfast.

"What's the matter with you?" Jade raised her brow as she shoved a piece of sausage into her mouth, looking into to Paige's bothered face.

"Y'all peep how Dante's been cooped up with the new girl lately?"

"Yea and?" Natalia, Dante's feisty Latin girl asked as she scrambled cheese eggs she was making for Dante.

"I'm not sure if I like it."

"Oh, come on girl don't be jealous. Dante did that to all of us remember. That's just him breakin' her in." Jade waved her off.

"I don't think it's like that." Paige shook her head. She went back to the words Dante said to Sasha, him comparing her to the rest of them. It made her nervous, even if he was just comparing cooking skills. "She's really feelin' herself."

"Don't we all when we get with him?" Jade reminded her.

"Shit, I know I do." Natalia and Jade high fived each other but Paige still found nothing funny. Just then Sasha entered in in Nala's white silk robe with just a thong on underneath. The girls turned to her with

155

their eyebrows raised. No one has ever worn Nala's robe, not even if Dante had them in their bedroom. Ever.

"Good morning girls." Sasha smiled at them unbothered by their surprised looks.

"Well good morning." Paige looked her up and down as Sasha made her way to the refrigerator to retrieve ingredients for Dante's breakfast. "You're especially chipper this morning."

"Well that's what happens when you wake up with the man of your dreams right girls?" She said placing bacon and eggs on the counter. "Mmm, that smells delicious." Sasha looked down at the plate that was decorated with eggs, sausage and waffles with strawberries with powdered sugar on top.

"It's Dante's favorite." Natalia beamed. "I figured I'd make his breakfast AND be this morning."

"I don't think he has a taste for either one, he asked me to make him breakfast this morning." Sasha began to chop up some potatoes. "But you can see if he'd like that instead.

"I'm sure he'd prefer it." Natalia smirked as she placed his food on a tray with orange juice and his morning paper. Natalia disappeared from the kitchen and Jade and Paige stayed silent as Sasha went on to prepare Dante's meal with a wide smile on her face. Natalia knocked on the door and waited anxiously for Dante to answer. Dante opened the door shirtless and wet with a towel wrapped around him.

"Good morning Dante." She kissed his cheek.

"Good morning." He looked down at the tray of food and raised his brow. "Wow, Sasha works fast."

"No boo I made this. I always make you breakfast on Saturday morning before our workout, remember?" She reminded him.

"Oh, that's right. Well this morning, I going to be eating what Sasha's making for me instead but thank you Natty. It looks awesome." He kissed her forehead. "You're always thinkin' of me."

"Of course I'm always thinkin' about you." She put on her best smile to hide her disappointment from him rejecting her meal. "So," she smirked, "even though you don't want breakfast, what about our morning workout?" Dante smirked back at her and nodded.

"I can't I have a full day." He rubbed her shoulder. "But I'll make it up to you soon, okay?"

"Alright Dante." She smiled and he planted a kiss on her cheek. "Have a good day."

"I'll see you later." He shut the door and she pouted as she made her way back towards the grand staircase and into the kitchen just as Sasha placed the last of the bacon she fried on to Dante's plate of grits, cheese eggs and fried potatoes.

"I tried to tell you." Sasha smirked.

"It's fine. He said he's going to do somethin' special with me soon so it's all good." Natalia faked another smile.

"Good for you. Well if you'll excuse me, I don't want to his food to get cold so, I gotta go. Don't let that

157

breakfast go to waste. Maybe you girls can split it." Sasha threw over her shoulder as exited the kitchen, the white robe flowing beautifully behind her.

All alone in the small cabin I'm now confined to for the rest of my life, I the King have nothing but time to analyze the rise and demise of my own empire. Had it been the blood thirst desire for power that controlled my morale and forced me to betray the only ones who love me? Or was it the failure of my forefathers that fueled me to make sure I could have absolute and total control all things around me and people? All these questions echo in the crevices of my brain, though I try to ignore them. But I cannot. Time is all I have now to think of these things. Time. It is the only thing on my side. Or is it?

Paulie sat quietly in his cell, deep into the novel about a king named Eli in deep despair over the loss of his kingdom. He shook his head as he read the kings confessions of sad thoughts and resentful feelings. He couldn't help but relate. He was alone, had been betrayed and was left with nothing but his memories and choices to sift through. He knew plenty of those choices a lead him to his permanently barred cage and that al in all, he was grateful that the God had still sparred his life.

"Sir." Sebastian cleared his throat as he approached Paulie's cell. "Sorry to disturb you."

"Not disturbance at all." Paulie looked up from his book and removed his glasses. "I trust that you have that information I requested?"

"Not exactly sir, I found the address belonging to a Nala Wilson and it happens to be your address."

"Right, I knew that."

"But that was all I found. There have been no recent sightings of her in the past two weeks on the premises." Paulie's eyes sparked with curiosity.

"Surely she's flown to another country. Dante did tell me of her newfound love for fashion and exploring different cultures to get her creative juices flowing."

"There is no trace of boarding passes. Not even a train or bus ticket attached to her name. The private jet has been used quite a bit but not by her. A group of women have accompanied your son on it numerous times but according to the pilot, none of them were Nala." Fire hot as lava flowed throughout Paulie's body as he sat still and replayed the conversation he and Dante shared. *Dante lied right to my face about Nala...but why? And who are those whores he's parading around my house?*
"Sir?" Paulie snapped out his thoughts.

"Just keep me up to date with everything you find out."

"Of course." Sebastian nodded before he left Paulie alone with his book, but Paulie was no longer interested in his book. He was beginning to wonder where Nala was.

"Aye man, this was one of the best scores we've had in a minute." Don pulled up to the curb to let Cole out so he could walk the short path home. "Lester Givens was very generous."

"Shit, with all that money, I'm glad he could be. Thanks for the ride as usual homie." Cole slapped hands with Don.

"And I'm foreal about Bailey Estates. Give it another thought. We could hit bigger than this."

"Yea I will." Cole exited the car with a book bag on his back. They slapped hands again and Don pulled away from the curb as Cole started towards the house. He seemed to be power walking, all too excited to get back to her. The streetlights flickered on as he made his way through the streets and the night freaks began to come out. A feeling of relief came over him once he saw the lights of the house shining through the blinds. Cole opened the in time to see her placing a bowl filled with creamy mac and cheese on the table. "Damn I was not expecting this." He set his bag down at the door and they met halfway for a hug. Cole wrapped his arms Nala's frame and squeezed her as he placed a gentle kiss on her, just as he did before he left.

"I missed you." She confessed.

"I missed you too." He confirmed kissing her lips again before she took his hand and lead him over to the table where she had his food hot and waiting for him. He sat down and gazed at the baked chicken breast with broccoli and mac and cheese, his stomach rejoicing. "Thank you." He leaned over and planted another kiss on her. They said prayer and dug in. His taste buds danced as he looked over her, Nala quietly eating her food. Cole placed his hand on her thigh, causing her to look up from her plate. She gave him a small smile and he returned one as well. "I'on like it when you quiet like this La. Where's the girl who loves to ask twenty-one questions?" Cole shook his head and touched her chin.

"I don't mean to be." She pushed back the thought of telling Cole about what happened yesterday. He had just returned home so she didn't want to hit him with the news just yet.

"As long as you're okay." Cole stared into her eyes for assurance.

"Yea." Nala put forth her best grin and Cole could see right through it. She was hiding something, but he decided he wouldn't press her about it. After dinner, Cole offered to the dishes but Nala insisted that he shower and chill, so he took her suggestion and did so. She waited for him on the couch as she found an action movie for them to watch. Cole emerged from the bathroom dressed in his usual sweatpants and beater, smelling all too good. Nala reached her arms out to him and he fell into them, resting his head on her chest. She massaged his back and arms as he listened to her gentle beating heart, trying his hardest not to fall asleep to its harmonious rhythm. Nala looked down and smiled softy at his sleeping face. She kissed his head and went back to watching the movie. *Tomorrow. I'll tell him tomorrow.*

Sweat dropped from Cole's forehead as he ran through the enormous mansion, kicking open doors and pointing his gold covered gun at whatever was in front of him. He could hear Nala screaming out in pain as she cried for him. Up the round staircase he went as her screams became terrifyingly louder, tears coming to his eyes. "Cole please help me!" He heard her desperate plea as he bolted towards a door down a long dark hallway, police sirens wailing and red and blue lights blinding his path. He felt as if the door was moving further away from him the harder, he ran to get to it. He finally made it, bursting through the door in time to see Nala reaching for him with a smile. Suddenly, the loud bang of a gun went off. The smile faded from her lips as she gasped. Tears cascaded from her face as she slowly fell to her knees, Dante's gun sizzling with smoke and a devilish grin on his face. Dante then pointed his gun at Cole, prompting Cole to point his back at him. He heard a click and felt a gun being pressed firmly into his skull. He turned his head to the side, Vanessa wearing the same evil smile as Dante. Cole looked back at Nala's limp body on the floor and closed his eyes before the loud bang of a gun went off.

Cole's eyes shot open. The living was dark with the tv on a low hum, Nala resting on top of his chest. He scooped her up in his arms and walked inside the bedroom, laying her under the covers before he went to turn off the tv. He returned to the room and joined her in bed, staring up at the ceiling as the dream replayed repeatedly. Nala felt for his arm and once she found it, she wrapped it around herself, pressing her body on his so he would hold her tighter. Cole did just as she wanted and planted a few kisses on her neck. He closed his eyes to fall asleep again but to no avail. Dante and Vanessa's smiling faces were all he could see.

17.

What Had Happened Was

Nala laid awake in the early morning watching Cole as he slept. He looked bothered and uncomfortable even as he held her body against his. He was so busy taking notice she was being quiet she realized he didn't say much either last night. He took a long breath and sighed. "You been up for a minute now just starin' at me. I know I'm not that good lookin'. What's wrong?" He looked down at her, seeing she was surprised he was awake.

"You look good to me."

"Maybe but I can tell just by lookin' at you somethin's up. So, what's up?" He touched her face. She swallowed hard as she stared deep into his eyes and tried to gather the courage to tell him everything but where to start? Dante or Vanessa? He waited patiently as she said nothing, just looking up into his eyes. "Would it make you feel better if I told you where I was? Is that what's bothering you?"

"I'm just afraid if you tell me where you were, then that just might make what I have to tell you ten times worse."

"Then you might as well just tell me whatever it is." Cole suggested but Nala was still silent. "You didn't hang out with Brittany and-"

"Oh please! WAY off the mark." She looked at him appalled.

"I just had to ask, you joked about it."

"But you of all people should know I would never do that."

"Well then tell me what it is Nala." He sat up on his hand with hardness in his voice.

"Dante let me know he's coming to find me if I don't go to him. I don't think he's playin' either." Nala raised her brow as Cole laughed.

"He doesn't scare me at all. That's what's got you shook?" Nala sat up and touched her shoulder against Cole's.

"That and we had a visitor while you were gone. A detective named Vanessa came around here askin' about you." Cole's heart pounded deep in his chest as the news sent a panic through his body he hadn't felt in a while. Nala could see the shift in his eyes as he sat still a stone. "She spoke to Bashi, Brittany and me-"

"Did Brittany say anything?"

"Surprisingly, no. She still thinks you're a mean man but she had your back." Nala kissed Cole's shoulder as he continued to sit mum to himself. Too many thoughts were running rapid through his brain and he was trying to figure out what to handle first. Dante was a small problem to him. But Vanessa was a growing problem and the fact that she was so close to where he laid his head did not sit right with him. He was incredibly careful, doing all the things necessary to keep anyone like her away from him. So how did she get so close? "Hey," Nala touched

Cole's face and he broke away from his thoughts, "Can you say somethin'?" She raised her brow.

"Damn..." He finally spoke as he got up off the bed and reached for his hoodie and placed it over his head.

"Where are you goin'?" Nala sat up on her knees as she watched him slip his shoes.

"I gotta go talk to Bashi, can you hold off right here for a little?"

"I can but I honestly don't think it's a good idea for you-" Cole kissed her lips as he secured his gun in his hoodie.

"I'm just goin' up the street. I don't want you to start worrying about me just because some cop came around here askin' questions. Just chill and I'll be back." He shut the bedroom door behind him.

"Someone has to worry about you..." she mumbled looking down at her silent phone.

Dante stood before the grand mirror in the bathroom, admiring his firm chest and chiseled abs before checking his phone again to see if Nala had given in to his warning. Sasha watched him from the Jacuzzi tub she was soaking in, smoking her morning blunt, happiness covering her entire being. The past few days had been full of everything he promised when they first met. She was waking up to kisses from him every morning, shopping sprees, expensive pamper treatments and getting a good nights after rounds of passionate fire filled sex. He was spoiling her bad and he knew it. It was all a part of his plan. He caught her wanting stare in the mirror and grinned hard. She was doing exactly what he wanted her to.

"You know," Dante turned around, "I enjoy your company. It's rare for me to just enjoy one woman."

"I'm a very rare woman." She blew smoke his way as he walked over to her and sat on the edge of the bathtub.

"Clearly."

"I'm starting to feel the animosity from the other girls. I think they're threatened by me."

"You're beautiful, loyal and willing to do more than cook my meals and spend my money. You want to help me." He took the blunt from her and puffed hard, "that's more than I can say about the others. They should feel threatened."

"So why have them? I'm all you need Dante. I can do everything they do ten times better and you'll never have to question me." He nodded and exhaled his smoke in her face, her sniffing up as much of the fumes as she could. Dante placed his hand on her neck and brought her closer to him, moving some loose strands of hair from her face.

"I know but don't you worry about them, worry about us." She beamed at the way he spoke of them as if they were a unit. "I've given my special girl a special task. And I gave it to you cause, I know you can handle it. You ready to start?"

168

"I've been ready." Dante's free hand disappeared under the water and she moaned at touch as they stared into one another.

"That's what I love to hear."

Vanessa stared hard into her computer screen fixated on the picture of Cole she had up on her computer. She memorized his file front and back and knowing everything about him from his mother's drug addiction to his anger management problems down to where his grandmother rested her head. Yet, she could not find him. Vanessa groaned and slammed her head onto her desk, causing Dave to look up from his station.

"Care to explain?"

"Yes, I want an explanation as to how taxpayer's dollars go to all this technology that can track terrorist in caves yet my ass can't find a guy that's been hiding underneath our noses for the past two years. This doesn't make sense to me." She shook her head as she refocused on his handsome face.

"Why are you so obsessed with this guy?"

"See when a man is one hundred percent into his job, he's confident and manly. Let a woman share the same passion and she's obsessed and crazy. This is exactly why we need a female president."

"A female president isn't gonna make double standards go away, that'll probably make things worse." Vanessa rolled her eyes at him. "I was just kidding." He tossed a balled-up piece of paper her way and she dodged it. "I just think you need to relax. They about to cold case him anyway."

"I know that Dave, but I SAW him, I KNOW I did. He was at that grocery store, I looked him dead in the eyes." She expressed deeply as she took another look into his brown eyes on the computer. "It was him...I felt it."

"If it was him then what stopped you?"

"Oh come on Dave," Vanessa leaned back in her chair, "you now Captain's motto, "Attest then arrest." I needed actual physical proof it was him."

"That's cause the city doesn't want any lawsuits. Think about it. How would you feel if your brother were mistakenly arrested for somethin' so serious? You'd bring hell and high water. All these wrongful deaths that have been happening at the hands of the law lately, we gotta be careful." Vanessa twirled in her chair as she listened to Dave's lecture. He was always the logical one of the two.

"Okay so if you were me, what would you do?"

"I'd give up." Dave shrugged his shoulders and Vanessa rolled her eyes.

"Somethin' that doesn't require me to be a pussy."

"Well maybe you need to put yourself in his shoes. Think like a criminal. How would you survive?"

"No one can survive completely on their own out in this world, especially if they're a high-profile criminal. Not unless..." Vanessa tapped her manicured nails against her woodened desk as her unsuccessful visit to the broken-down neighborhood popped up into her head.

"Unless?" Dave raised his brow as he watched a surprised smile creep onto her face.

"Unless you have people helping you. Thank you, Dave. You're not as dumb as you act." Vanessa snatched her jacket off the back of her chair and kissed Dave's cheek before making her way out the precinct.

18.

Deception

Cole opened the door to the restaurant to find Bashi warming up the grill as he danced to some Al Green. Cole laughed as he watched Bashi bounce to the music and Bashi turned around with a wide smile, all too happy to see Cole alive and well.

"Someone is especially happy this morning." Cole and Bashi shared a hug.

"It's always a good day when the Lord wakes you up. He woke you up early I see."

"It's kinda hard to stay sleep with everything goin' on right now." Cole wiped his hands down his face before leaning on the counter.

"I'm glad Nala told yout though." Bashi raised his brows and nodded his head, "She was afraid of how you might've reacted."

"I don't even know how to react right now."

" She feels so bad for you Cole."

"But I don't want her to, it's life." Cole shrugged.

"She cares." Bashi pointed to him before reaching into his cooler to grab some ingredients for a hearty breakfast. "And that is hard to come by these days." Cole nodded. "And I'm sure she's uneasy with Dante threating her. She could be worried about what would happen if he were to discover this relationship you two share."

"Man, I ain't worried about him." Cole stood up firmly. "Whenever he's ready, I'm ready." The image of Nala's bruised body was still stitched into his brain. He was never letting that go. "It's this detective I'm worried bout. Vanessa."

"Ah yes the nosy young woman who came snoopin' around here lookin' for you."

"Yea but when I first met her, she told me her name was Gloria." Bashi turned to Cole before he placed two steaks on the grill. "When I went to the grocery store, I did my usual thing. Rode through where the cameras couldn't see me, kept my head low, hood up and said nothin' to no one. She checked me out in line and was askin' me all types of questions." Cole laughed to himself and Bashi moved about behind the counter grabbing and mixing things.

"Mm, seems to me she plans on pushing you out son. So," Bashi stopped his movements to face Cole, "what is it you plan to do about it?"

Sasha made her way down the grand stairs in gold six-inch heels, tight jeans and a white crop top, her driver waiting at outside to escort her to the precinct. Dante had given her specific instructions on what to do, who to talk to and how to act to get the information he wanted. She made sure she was on point.

"Well don't you look nice." Paige raised her brow as she met Sasha at the bottom of the staircase. "Where you off to?

"Thanks, Dante bought the shoes. He has such great taste. He wanted me to look extra scrumptious for today's errands. " Sasha flipped her hair and looked Paige up and down who was dressed in shorts and a black tank top. "Any plans for yourself today?"

"I'm not sure, Dante has asked that I come see him." Paige lied just to see the disgust on Sasha's face. "So, I'm sure I'll be occupied while you're gone. Have fun on your errands." Paige smirked. Sasha laughed and tossed her hair out her view to slide her dark designer shades onto her face.

"Of course I will honey. Try not to bore Dante while I'm away." Sasha switched as the maid at the front door handed over her purse before exiting the mansion. Paige stomped up the steps and off down the hall to Dante's room she went.

"There's no way I'm gonna let some little girl come in here think she has spot over me." Paige stood before his door and undressed herself till she was completely naked. She didn't even bother to knock on the door as she opened it and slipped inside. She tip-toed to the bathroom where Dante was showering alone with classical violin music playing in the background. Paige stepped into the steam filled bathroom and watched Dante for a second as he lathered his body and hummed along with the symphony. She bit her lip at the way the water caressed his flexing muscles. Paige opened the door to the shower and stepped inside. Dante turned around, a surprised smile popping up on to his face.

"This is a pleasant surprise." He spoke as Paige shut the door.

"I'm sure it is." She took his washcloth and began to wash his chest for him as she kissed his neck. "I've been missing you Dante. I never have to go this long without seeing you."

"I'm sorry baby but I've just been dealing with a few things. You know I have to work hard to keep my girls comfortable."

"Yea well Sasha seems to be really comfortable." Dante chuckled as she continued to wash him.

"She's new, she needs to feel comfortable. All of you went through the same thing."

"I know but-" Dante kissed her lips.

"Your jealousy is cute." Paige rolled her eyes and he brought her face closer to his.

"I'm not jealous." He kissed her lips again, slow and soft.

"Yes, you are." He rubbed her middle and she gasped as he began to gently massage her, her still running the soapy cloth over his glistening dark skin. "I like it though. Let's me know you're committed to me." She moaned again as he slid a finger inside her. "You are committed to me, right?

"Yes." She whispered as he removed his finger.

"So, if there comes a time and I need you to handle somethin' for me, I can trust you?"

"Of course you can Dante." She sucked his fingers. "You know you can." Paige bent over and invited him to drown in her pool love she only opened for him.

176

Nala paced back and forth in the living room with her gun in her fingers, anxiously waiting to hear from Cole or see him come through the front door. He'd been gone for almost thirty minutes now and her nerves became worse with each minute that passed. She heard a car door slam outside and ran over to the window to peek out the blinds. Her stomach dropped at the sight of Vanessa looking around the neighborhood with dark black shades covering her face and her hands on her hips. Vanessa turned to the direction of Bashi's restaurant and Nala quickly backed away from the blinds and took her phone out, contemplating on if she should call Cole or not.

"Damn Bashi, this looks amazing." Cole sat at the table as Bashi placed two plates of steak, cheesy eggs, grits and biscuits down before him. "Nala's gon be jealous."

"I doubt that. Nala loves her fruit."

"That's why you started keepin strawberries and what not around."

"Can't cater to just you anymore." Bashi laughed as Cole stood from his chair.

"I'ma go wash my hands." Cole disappeared in the back and the bell rang loudly, Bashi turning to see who it is.

"Hi there." Vanessa smiled at him. "Remember me?"

"Ms. Frazier, right?"

"Right." She looked down at the table decorated with two plates and looked about the restaurant. "Having a big breakfast this morning I see." Bashi looked down at the two place settings he made and laughed nervously.

"I know I'm a big man, but I can't eat this alone. I'm waiting for someone."

"If I knew such a well-cooked breakfast were being made for me, I'd be on time. Don't you just hate when people make you wait?" Vanessa walked up to counter, looking around the restaurant for any other signs of life.

"I'm a patient man I suppose." Bashi shrugged his shoulders, taking a quick glance towards the bathrooms.

"I wish I were. Long lines and being on hold bother me. But liars bother me even more." Vanessa looked him straight in the face. "Especially liars who lie right to my face."

"I couldn't agree more with you there. No one likes to be lied to." Bashi nodded his head and took a seat on his wooden stool.

"I have to be honest with you Bashi. For some strange reason, I feel like you lied to me. So, I'd like to give you a chance to ease my troubled mind. You weren't at the grocery store on the day I questioned you about. Your car was, but you weren't." She pointed to Bashi. "Am I right?"

"You know, you were much nicer the first time we met. You rang up my milk and apples and other things with a smile. Gloria, right?" Vanessa's eyes widened at the sound him using her undercover name. "I remember because my mother's name is Gloria and you had such a sweet spirit, just like her. I may have seemed a little off when you came in the other day because I could've sworn you worked at the grocery store. Meeting you this third time around?" he shook his head, "It's starting to feel like harassment. Perhaps your search isn't going as well as you'd hoped. I told you, if you're looking for criminals, head over to Griffin."

"Yea I heard you the first time. I just wanted to make sure you weren't trying to turn me away for the wrong reasons. I'm sorry if it seems like harassment but I just want to make sure you as well as everyone else is safe from this guy. Who needs a criminal on the loose right?"

"I guess. But I feel there are way more out there on the loose than the one you're lookin' for."

"Gotta take them down one by one." Vanessa leaned off the counter and looked back down at the two plates then back to Bashi. "Your friend is taking their sweet time huh?"

"They never are on time." Bashi laughed as he looked backed at the bathrooms again. Vanessa took notice, taking a glance over her shoulder at the bathrooms.

"You know what's worse than chasing a criminal?"

"Haven't got a clue." Bashi shook his head.

"Chasing a criminal who has people helping him stay hidden."

"If there is something you want to ask me, even if I've already answered it, you might as well ask it again." Bashi stepped down from the counter. "Cause, it seems like, you need some reassurance."

"Alright. I won't even pull up his picture cause I'm sure you've seen him. Are you helping or have recently seen Cole Thompson?" Just then the bell sounded and Nala appeared dressed her hoodie sweatpants as usual.

"There you are." Bashi smiled at her.

"Sorry I'm late." Nala softly spoke as she walked over to him and they hugged.

"Princess," Vanessa smiled, "you're looking well as usual."

"That's because she's been eatin' my good cookin'. She does a really good job around here, so I have to keep her fed you know." Bashi laughed. "Speaking of which your food is getting cold so come on." Bashi pulled out the chair and Nala took a seat. Bashi pulled Vanessa to the side as Nala closed her eyes and said a prayer for help and protection. "And once again Ms. Frazier, the answer is no. I'm sorry that I can't help you." Vanessa held her composure a defeat ran rapid inside her.

"I'm sorry too. You have my card if you need anything." Nala opened her eyes and took a bit of the warm cheesy eggs.

"I do. Thank you." Bashi opened the door for her and she stepped back out into the morning air. Bashi turned to Nala how who was chewing her food, quietly staring out the window and watching

Vanessa slowly walk past the restaurant. Vanessa looked up at the sky before getting into her car and could see dark clouds gathering. It was turning into a gloomy day. Simply perfect to match her mood. Nala put the fork down, her stomach barely tolerating the eggs she'd just eaten. Cole slowly came out from the back room where the bathrooms were located, Nala being the first person he saw.

"Y'all okay?" Cole looked between Bashi and Nala.

"I think we're good for now." Bashi looked through the blinds to see Vanessa driving away. "But I think you two needs to start discussing some options. And by options, I mean finding any place other than here."

"Right." Cole sat down next to Nala at the table as Bashi locked the store, turned off the lights and closed all the blinds as well. He sat down in an extra chair at the table and slid the untouched plate his way as Nala handed Cole his rightful dish. Bashi brought Nala her usual bowl of fruit. "Cole, I trust you have connections that may be able to find you housing?"

"It could take a couple days but I'm sure they could hook me up with something. It'll just be a little harder without you Bashi." Cole shook his head, completely unprepared for this conversation. He never thought that he would have to plan an escape route for the life he'd grown accustomed to living to. It wasn't perfect but it was his.

"I know but I'll always be here. I may even have a friend who can help get you your own ride."

"Nah," Cole shook his head as he wiped his mouth with his napkin, "I think a car is too dangerous for me to be driving around in right now."

"I could drive. Not like the police suspect me of anything." Nala chimed in and Cole placed his hand on her thigh under the table.

"That's true." Cole agreed.

"I'll need a day or two to talk to him. In the meantime, I think you outta lay real low Cole."

Sasha switched her hips to the front desk where an older man with a white and gray mustache was busy reading the paper.

"Excuse me," Sasha removed her sunglasses from her face to reveal fake tears she worked hard to produce. "Is Detective Eddie Martinez available?" The older man sympathized with her and led her to an office where a handsome young Spanish detective was writing quietly at his desk. His eyes fell on her chocolate face and he was instantly attracted to her. She could see it through her tear-filled eyes.

"Hi, I'm Detective Martinez but you can call me Eddie. How can I help you Miss?" He handed her a tissue.

"You can call me Sasha." She patted her eyes dry as she took a seat the comfy office chair.

"What's going on Sasha?"

182

"I haven't heard from my sister in about two weeks now and I'm really starting worry." She sniffled.

"Okay what is her name and when was the last time you saw or heard from her?" Eddie clicked his pen ready to take notes.

"Nala Thompson. When we said good night to each other the night before I discovered she was one. We live together. She mentioned that she had had a really bad day and wanted to go to bed early."

"Why wait so long to come in and speak to someone?" Eddie raised his brow.

"My sister is not exactly the most stable person. Her mother used drugs when she was pregnant with her, so her mind isn't completely together. She does this sometimes where she'll be gone for a few days and then she'll come back happy." Sasha sniffed again as Eddie wrote furiously on the paper.

"Is she on drugs?"

"To be honest she could be. Like I said she's so up and down with her moods, there's no telling." Sasha brought more tears to her brown eyes. "Listen Detective, our father is sick and if this were to get out that she's gone missing or worse, it just might kill him."

"I understand. I will be discreet about this as best as I can." Eddie nodded.

"Thank you. I tried to use my phone to see if I could track her phone but I'm not too good at those sorts of things."

"You should leave that up to us anyway. That's what your tax dollars pay for." Sasha smiled as she laughed inside at the thought of her having to pay for anything.

"I know, I was just afraid that she's in a place I don't want her to be. In the gutter or some dirty crack house."

"Let's hope not." He gave her a soft smile.

"Again, I'm afraid if this gets to my father, only the worse will happen. Do you think with the information you find that I can try looking for her first?"

"Unfortunately, I can't let you do that Sasha. That'd be going against my job rules and putting you in danger."

"I know but," she touched his hand "she's my sister and I'll do anything to protect her. If I find she's really in trouble and not just off in one of her moods, then I promise, I will call you. But just give me a chance first...please?"

The rain outside pounded against the window as Cole looked at Nala's back. She hadn't said anything since they came home from Bashi's. She took a nap, got up and made dinner, Cole did the dishes and right back to bed she went. The thunder rolled hard as Dante slammed his bedroom door shut to find Sasha waiting in red lace lingerie laying in the middle of the bed. He smirked as she sat up on her knees. The lightening flashed and Cole rolled onto his side and began to rub Nala's thigh. She turned to him.

"That smile on your face says you've had a productive day." Sasha reached for Dante's belt buckle as he unbuttoned his shirt.

"That it was. And your excitement to see me isn't just because now you can finally take my pants off, I hope?"

"Of course not." She leaned up and kissed his lips. Cole moved closer to her and kissed her shoulder as he looked into her eyes.

"You okay?" He kissed her skin again. She said nothing as their eyes stayed connected. "I know you're not." He pulled her closer and wrapped his arm around her. "But I gotchu." He kissed her lips softly.

"How long will it take for him to find out her exact location?" Dante moaned as Sasha ran her tongue along his shaft.

"He told me to come back tomorrow morning and he'll have it for me. I told you I'd get everything you need baby."

"That's my girl." He gripped her hair as she went deeper on him.

"I'ma protect you La. You don't have to be scared with me." He reassured her with more kisses and touched her face. She searched his eyes to find any reason to have doubt in him, but she couldn't. She simply nodded her head.

19.

Never Judge a Book by Its Cover

"You know today is the third day?" Nala spoke as she continued to lay in Cole's arms. Last night's storm was finally passing, lighting no longer striking the sky and the thunder was now soft ripples of rumbling.

"I know," he looked down at her, " but I told you don't have to be scared."

"I'm not scared. I'm just anxious. We got lucky with Vanessa but I'm not sure if it'll be the same way with Dante." She sat up on her arm and rubbed Cole's chest. "He's smart. Not so much street smart but he knows how to use his charm and resources to get what he wants." Nala knew from her own experience just how strong Dante's power of manipulation was. Always using his name, among other things, just to have his way. She just knew he was up to something.

"You think he knows Vanessa?"

"No. If he did, he would've been here already or she woulda snatched me up. What's up with this chick? She like you or somethin'?" Cole chuckled as his fingers roamed across Nala's thigh.

"She might. I don't even know where she came from."

"Is that your thing? Random girls come across you and you just hypnotize them into liking you?" Nala and Cole laughed as she played in his wild bush.

"Only pretty ones with crazy ex boyfriends." Nala softly hit his chest and he pulled her down to his eye level. She giggled as he kissed her lips and he continued to rub on her thighs. "What can I do to make you feel better about all this? I don't like when this face of yours is pouty or quiet."

"If you and I make an actual plan together. One that can at least get us out of here by the morning." Nala traced his lips with her finger, infatuated with how pink and soft they were.

"By morning?" Cole raised his brow and Nala nodded her head.

"We just move need to move around, go to a motel or somethin simple with a roof just until one of your or Bashi's connections come through. I don't think we should wait though. " Cole let go of Nala and turned on the small lamp by his bedside.

"Hand me the black duffle bag in the closet." Nala removed the covers from her body and retrieved the bag that Cole asked her for. She recalled him bringing it in the house with him the night he returned but she never saw it after. It had some weight to it, so her curiosity rose as she set the bag before him. Cole peeked over at her before he unzipped the duffle bag and revealed some women's clothing and money. Her mouth fell open as Cole fully spilled the contents of the bag on the bed.

"Cole, what the hell? Where did you get this stuff?" She picked up one of the tank tops, half surprised to see it but also rejoicing that she had a few new clothes to wear.

"I stole it." Her mouth fell open again at his confession and he laughed. "Come on, don't make that face like you're totally surprised."

"I mean I'm not but, damn. I wasn't expecting to see all this money." Her eyes stayed on the pool of green paper that mostly had Ben and Andrew's faces printed on them.

"I've made more but trust me, I didn't think I was gonna make out this well either." Cole began to take up the money and count it. Nala sat quietly in the middle of the bed as she watched him count and put the money into piles.

"Can I help you?" He patted an open spot next to him. She crawled to the spot, took up a handful of money and began to count. They put the money in piles of hundreds and then into to piles of thousands once they began to run out of room on the bed. Nala stared at the square pile of money they built in shock awe. "Whoever you took this from sure is gonna be pissed." She shook her head as Cole got behind her and wrapped his arms around her. "Hell, I would be."

"Nah, they won't miss it. Trust me, five thousand dollars is like pocket change to them. They won't even notice it's gone." He shoved his face in her neck and breathed deeply before kissing it.

"Trust me, they'll notice it and they'll care. This is money we're talkin' about...six thousand four hundred and seven dollars' worth. I know you ain't do this by yourself either so technically you and whoever you hit the lick with, took over twelve g's."

"Don't worry about that. We've got some money to get us started." He gave her body a light squeeze and kissed her cheek. "And we can leave in the morning, just like you want." Cole leaned back against the wall still holding Nala close to him as she rested her head back on his shoulder. He stared down at the stack of money and hoped Nala was wrong about Lester's side chick noticing her treasures missing. He didn't have time to worry about anyone else on his back.

"This is how you've been able to stay hidden all this time. You go on your trips and give the money to Bashi to pay the bills so there's no paper trail behind you." All of Bashi's secrecy and small lies began to make perfect sense to her. He was protecting Cole.

"Yes mam."

"Sweet Bashi...I'm going to miss him."

"Me too." Cole kissed her cheek as she played with his fingers and he stared out at the wall in front of him. "Me too..."

The bell sounded and Bashi turned around from the grill to see who his unexpected customer was. The rain was pouring so hard outside that not even the neighborhood druggie crew was out and about. His eyes fell upon a young man who was dressed in a hoodie with a black duffle bag strapped over his shoulder.

"It's comin' down out there ain't it son?" Cole shook himself and removed his hood from his head.

190

"Like you wouldn't believe. I'm glad you're open this late."

"Yea I don't do much sleeping anyway. You hungry?"

"I could eat. Whatchu got on the menu?" Cole walked up to the counter.

"Well, I got burgers, hot dogs, chicken wings, chicken breast-"

"All of that sounds good." Cole held his stomach as it growled. "You can throw down whatever you want." Bashi chuckled.

"Well, take a seat young man. Judging by that hair on your chin, I'd say you're old enough for a brew." Bashi opened a beer as he took a careful look at Cole, wondering where he had seen him before. He set it on the counter and opened another one for himself.

"Thank you." They both raised their beers to each and drank from them. "This is a nice spot you have here." Cole looked around at the well-kept restaurant. There were four tables with chairs and two green booths alongside the wall. On the back wall were shelves stocked with toiletries such as toothpaste, deodorant, shampoo and conditioner, socks and more.

"Old guy like me tries his best."

"My grandma says you're only as old as you make yourself feel. She's pushin' seventy but she swears she's thirty-five or somethin'." They both laughed and Bashi nodded.

"That's a great mantra, I outta remember that. So," Bashi pulled some things out from his cooler, "what are you doin' out in the rain? Especially at a time like this?" Cole stood quietly as he took another drink from his beer and tried to think of something to say. He had been on the run for quite some time and now felt he was far enough from the chaos to try and find a place to lay his head for a while.

"I just moved here. Well, technically, I'm still lookin for a place."

"Shoot, you ain't gon' find much here. Just a bunch of riff raff who cause nothin' but noise and trouble." Bashi spoke as he stood over the grill, sizzling sounds animating his words and a wonderful aroma came creeping around Cole's nose.

"Damn, it's rough neighborhood like that? Why are you still here then?"

"This is home. I grew up here, my restaurant is here...kind of shitty but it's home, ya know?"

"Yea..." Cole took a seat at one of the tables as Bashi continued to whip up a hearty meal. He removed his wet hoodie from his shoulders and sat it on top of his bag. He laughed at the way Bashi moved to and fro with the jazz music playing, humming and dancing as he went about.

"So where is home for you? Or was since you're on a venture to find a new one."

"It's hard to say really. I've moved around so much I don't think I've ever really had a home." Cole tried to keep his answer as generic as possible. Bashi seemed like a cool guy but the way he was speaking

192

on the neighborhood made Cole feel like Bashi would call the police on him in a heartbeat.

"Almost wish I could say the same for myself."

"You never wanted to get out of here?" Bashi shrugged his shoulders.

"I've had my moments where I thought maybe I could go out and venture the world, start a new life but it just never fully pulled me out. Especially when there's so many memories here. Besides, I can handle this neighborhood. You all can have the rest of this crazy world." Bashi chuckled as he left the grill and took a seat on a wooden stool that was behind the counter. He picked up his paper and waved it in the air. "I'll watch the madness from the sidelines. All these fools runnin' around committin' crimes to people who ain't never done nothin' to 'em. Just selfish and poorly raised don't ya think? " He chuckled again as he opened his paper and Cole swallowed hard. "Food will be done here shortly." Bashi's eyes scanned the paper as Cole continued to sit quiet so that he wouldn't say anything to incriminate himself. He looked at the grill contemplating if he should hurry and finish his beer or wait for the meal Bashi was preparing for him. Cole looked out to the wet streets and Bashi looked over his newspaper at him, trying to remember where he knew him from. He obviously wasn't from any place around Silverdale, but he felt as if he'd already met him before. Cole looked back to the beer between his hands, face deep in what Bashi believed was concern and exhaustion. He wondered when the last time he took a real shower and slept. The way his face hardened, Bashi knew for sure he had seen the young man before. "So," Bashi closed his paper and Cole brought his face up from his beer, "Got any young ones?" Bashi got up from his stool and went back over to the grill as Cole laughed and shook his head.

"Man, none that I know of. Besides, I don't have a lady to give me any."

"Aww come on, handsome young fella like yourself should have a special young lady somewhere." Cole shook his head again, thinking about his most recent relationship and its disastrous end.

"I ain't never been that lucky. Thought I was but you know, life happens."

"I know all about that, trust me." Bashi turned off his grill and grabbed two plates to fill up with food. "Love is so precious and so damn need yet it's such a task to find someone who values it." Bashi came from behind the counter and set the two plates filled with rice, chicken and mixed vegetables on the table, Cole's stomach rejoiced loudly enough for Bashi to hear. "But it's real. It's out there." Bashi went to grab two more beers from his cooler and when he turned to return to the table, he could see that Cole was praying over his food quietly. Once he finished, Bashi joined him at the table and they began to eat. Cole's belly thanked him for the warm meal as he shoved piles of the tasty mix into his mouth. "I have more on the grill if you want more when you're done bulldozing it down your throat." Bashi smiled before biting into his own food. Cole nodded and continued to devour the delicious rice into his mouth. He was starving and he figured the quicker he ate, the quicker he could get out of there.

"This is pretty good." Cole finally slowed his pace of eating.

"Wish I said I came up with it. Evie, my late wife, loved to cook this on Friday's so she called it her "Friday Feel Good" meal."

"Well it certainly lives up to its name." Cole leaned back in his chair and rubbed his stomach, letting his food settle as he shuffled the idea of getting a second plate.

"I thought you could use it." Bashi nodded his head in agreement and wiped his mouth with a napkin. He and Cole made eye contact for some seconds and Cole shifted uncomfortably in his chair. Bashi looked down at the black duffle bag on the floor close to Cole and Cole moved again, causing the scope of his gun on his waist to flash Bashi. Bashi chuckled setting his fork down onto his plate. "I never did catch your name young man?" Bashi wiped his mouth with napkin.

"Andre." Cole answered.

"Nice to meet you Andre, I'm Foo Boo." Cole raised his eye at the odd name as Bashi leaned forward with one hand out and smiled.

"Nice to meet you." Cole took his hand. Suddenly Bashi's grip tightened on Cole and he pulled small gun from inside his vest pocket, pointing it towards Cole's chest. Cole's eyes batted with disbelief as he looked between the old man and the gun.

"You might have thought because of the gray hairs resting on top my head and curled up in my beard you could fool me but I can assure you, I'm no old

fool young man." Bashi looked hard into Cole's face. "Now, I wanna give a chance to redeem yourself. When I let go of you, you'll remain calm and won't reach for that shiny piece of steel you have attached to your hip, right?" Cole nodded. After a short intense stare down Bashi let his hand go, still keeping his gun on Cole. "Now put your gun on the table."

"How do I know you won't shoot me once I do?" Cole raised his brow.

"Unless you give me a reason, I don't plan on it." Reluctantly, Cole pulled his gold gun from out his front pocket and laid it in the middle of the table before Bashi. Bashi nodded with satisfaction. "And now, I'm going to put my gun down with a firm belief you're not going to pick up yours." Bashi laid his gun next to Cole's and Cole relaxed. "One of the main keys to any relationship is trust. Trust is what we've just established here young man. Trust is nothing without the truth though. Can't trust someone if they lie to ya." Bashi ate from his plate.

"You're right."

"So, how about we restart this conversation?" Bashi wiped his mouth. "I never did catch your name young man?" They let out light laughs.

"Cole." He held out his hand to Bashi.

"I'm Bashi." They shook hands and Bashi nodded his head as he analyzed Cole's rough appearance. "I didn't recognize you at first Cole but now I see you. It's good you're growing your hair and beard out. It'll hide you more." Bashi went back to eating his food as Cole sat stunned in his seat.

"How'd you know it was me?"

"I'm old school. I still read the paper and watch the news channel. It's been a month or two since I heard anything about you though."

"I gotta say that's good to hear. I try not to listen too much to it. I just keep movin'." Cole went back to his food.

"Honestly, son, you look like you haven't stopped movin' in a while. Shoot, you made it all the way to Silverdale."

"I'm tryna move as far as possible away from this mess."

"All that movin', you ever stop to think about where you're goin'?" Bashi drank from his beer.

"No time to stop." Bashi nodded as Cole scooped up what was left of the rice. They sat in silence for some minutes as the rain continued to pound outside. Bashi looked at the soaked streets and then back to Cole.

"I have a small place down the street if you really need a place to rest. It's not much but it has a twin mattress, a tv, bathroom, kitchen, all the necessities. You're more than welcome to stay there til you figure out your next move son. " Cole rejoiced inside at the sound of sleeping on a bed, but his pride quickly punctured his joy.

"Look you don't have to do that. I'm grateful for you sharing a meal with me even though you know who I am."

"I'm sure you're not too bad. Besides, it ain't like you sellin' death on the streets like the rest of these fools. Just got a severe case of sticky fingers. Would you like another plate?" Bashi stood up with his own plate and grabbed Cole's.

"Please..." Cole couldn't believe he had an actual bed to lay in for the next few nights instead of a bus stop or bathroom. "Thank you...I really appreciate this." Bashi placed a fresh plate of food in front of Cole and took a seat with his own.

"Long as you don't take nothin' from me, you all right." They both let out loud and hearty laughs. "You know how to play Domino's young man?"

"Good morning." Paige dryly spoke as she walked into the kitchen to find Natalia painting her finger nails a plum color and Jade flipping through the morning paper at the table.

"What's so good about it?" Natalia scoffed as she blew on her wet nails.

"You woke up." Jade tossed over her paper.

"Yea but I woke up to nothing. No dick or no Dante. I don't know what his stupid obsession is with that little bitch, but I can't wait for it to be over." Natalia blew on her nails.

"She acts like she's his dick or somethin' the way she stays attached to him." Paige and Natalia laughed loudly as Jade shook her head. She didn't think Dante being with Sasha for so long was as big

198

of a deal as the girls were making it out to be. Dante always had his moments of favoritism every now and again, so she was sure he'd be back to putting the girls in rotation soon enough. Just then Sasha came into the kitchen dressed in a white thong with Nala's robe trailing behind her, silencing the chatter and laughter.

"Well damn. Don't stop the party just because I showed up." Sasha smirked walking up to the table.

"Good morning Sasha." Jade spoke.

"Good morning Jade. Glad to see somebody in here knows how to speak. Why you hoes so mum now?"

"Seniority little bitch. I ain't gotta speak to you." Natalia continued to blow on her nails.

"But don't think you can speak about me and I'm not gon say nothin'. Seniority or not, bitch."

"You know," Paige chimed in, "for someone who's barely been here a month, you sure are feelin' yourself."

"Are you mad because I've been here a shorter time and have Dante all to myself? Or are you mad cause you been here longer but Dante is feelin' me way more than you two bitter bitches put together?" Natalia let out a loud and very sarcastic laugh before speaking harsh unknown words in Spanish. "Bitch I don't speak that bullshit so I'm gonna take it as disrespect."

"Take it however you want to honey just don't take it lightly."

"Come on y'all can we not? It's too early in the morning for the pettiness." Jade rolled her eyes and went over to the coffee brewer to pour herself a cup.

"I serve petty round the clock so whenever you want your dose baby girl, let me know." Natalia smirked up at Sasha who was ready to fire back.

"Good morning ladies." A shirtless Dante smoothly strolled into the kitchen and Sasha swallowed the words she had planned for Natalia and decided to save them for another moment.

"Good morning Dante." They all spoke in sweet harmony as he walked over to Jade and gave her a light kiss before taking the cup of coffee she just prepared for herself.

"All of you look beautiful this morning." He pecked Paige and Natalia at the table.

"Well you know you always look good baby." Sasha stroked his ego before giving him a juicy tongue filled kiss, being sure to look at Natalia while doing so.

"Well thank you baby." Dante sipped from the hot coffee. "Go and get ready, we'll be leaving within the next hour." He tapped Sasha's ass to send her on her way.

"You're right love. WE have a busy day ahead of us." She kissed him once more. "Ladies, I'm sure we'll do this again."

"Can't wait." Natalia smiled. Once Sasha exited the kitchen, Natalia dropped her smile and rolled her eyes. "Dante, she got one more time to get slick with me before I cut her ass."

"Come on Natty, you're too pretty to be fightin'." Dante shook his head and laughed. "Besides, we have something to discuss as a family." Paige offered him her seat and began to massage his shoulders "As you all know, Nala has been gone for almost a month now. Has she tried to reach out to any of you?"

"Of course she hasn't. You know she wasn't too fond of us being around." Paige reminded him and Natalia agreed as Jade quietly re-poured herself a cup of coffee.

"I don't know how she was able to get out of here without a sound. It doesn't matter though. I'm doing everything I can to ensure her safety and bring her back."

"Yea well when she comes back, can we get rid of the fuckin' mutt?"

"Come on Natty," Dante chuckled, "Sasha is a good girl."

"We wouldn't know that the way she's been stuck up your ass." Paige planted a kiss on his cheek.

"Sasha and I are working on something together but you're right, I have been spending a lot of time with her. I hear you girls."

"So when can we expect to start getting some more time with you?" Jade finally spoke up as she walked over to the table.

"I just need y'all to give me a little bit of time to figure a couple things out and then I gotchu, I promise." All the girls made silent eye contact with each other, not sure what to make of Dante's promise. He could sense the worry in them. "Come on now, y'all been holdin' me down hard as hell and I'll make it up to you. Business is about to pick up in every way and I'm gonna need you all by my side to help make things run smoothly. I just need to hear you trust me." He pleaded to keep them on his team.

"We trust you." Paige draped her arms over his chest and kissed his cheek again. He grinned and held out his hands for Natalia and Jade to place their hands in. Jade and Natalia looked to each other before smiles crossed their faces.

"I trust you." Natalia placed her hand in his and he kissed it sweetly.

"I trust you too." Jade confirmed as he did the same to Jade and they all laughed together. But through those fake smiles and laughter, Dante couldn't see that one of them was planning to leave him if he didn't keep his promise, one had already betrayed him and the other...was going to die soon.

20.

We'll Meet Again

Sasha removed her sunglasses from her face as the air in the precinct cooled her glowing chocolate skin. Some of the uniformed men paused whatever task they were doing at the moment to catch quick sight of her hips and bare legs sway up to the front counter in the short white sundress she chose to hunt Nala with Dante in.

"Hi, is Mr. Eddie Martinez available?" She sweetly spoke to the older black woman who was occupying the desk this time.

"Sasha." She turned to see Eddie walking towards her with a manila folder in his hands.

"Good morning Mr. Martinez." Sasha turned to him.

"Good morning. You can come on back to my office." He led the way to his private room. "And remember," he shut the door behind him once they were inside alone, "you can call me Eddie." Eddie gently touched her shoulder.

"Right." She blushed taking a seat, trying to shake his charm. "Sorry my mind is all over the place right now with my sister, my father's illness and work...it's a lot to deal with." She sighed.

"I understand," he took a seat at his desk, "I'm sure it's difficult to try and handle all this while keeping your father out the loop. What's he battling if you don't mind me asking?"

"Cancer." Was the first thing she thought to say. "Lung cancer at that. He's the reason I wouldn't dare put my lips on a cigarette."

"Well I would hope not. They're too beautiful for you to carelessly use them in that manner." Eddie grinned, causing Sasha to blush again at the sight of his perfect white teeth. She brought her eyes back to his face and for once took a moment to really admire his handsome exotic features. His eyes were yummy hazel brown with feisty hints of green. His hair was dark, slicked back into a full man bun. His lips were juicy and rosy pink. He was staring back at her, admiring her just as hard as she was him.

"Thank you, Eddie," She took a deep breath to refocus on the task at hand. Dante was in the car outside and she didn't want to keep him waiting too long. "So, have you heard anything about my sister?" Eddie finally pulled his gaze from her face and shook his head.

"Right, well," He opened the manila folder and grabbed a pen, "I only have a few recent locations for her. She turns her location off and on, most likely turning them on once she finds a place with Wi-Fi. Now she hasn't traveled super far but she's definitely covered some ground. I have her pinned at this address here in Silverdale." He circled Cole's address with his red pen. "Do you have family or friends in that area? It's a pretty deserted and rundown there."

"Not that I know of." Sasha furrowed her eyebrows. "I can't imagine who she would know there."

"I doubt she would travel an hour and a half for no one or nothing. She must know someone. I picked up her phone records too." Eddie placed the phone records before her. "One number was pretty much the only one she had incoming or outgoing calls to. But there are two inconsistent numbers." He circled the two numbers on the paper. The number splashed all over the page belonged to Dante but the two Eddie circled made Sasha raise her brow. One she knew for sure who it belonged to, the other she had no clue. She scanned the date and time that belonged to the number she was familiar with and made a mental note of it.

"May I write this address down?" Sasha batted her eyes up at him.

"Of course, beautiful." His dimples flexed as he passed her his pad and pen.

"You flatter all the girls that come into your office like this?" Sasha peeked up at him as she wrote down the number that was odd to her on one slip and the address on another.

"Just you." She smiled as she placed both papers in her purse. "Sasha you're beautiful. I know that you're going through a lot and I hope I'm not being insensitive by asking you to join me for dinner or a drink some time?"

"That's extremely sweet of you Eddie but I'm not sure that would be a good idea. It's like you said, I have a lot goin' on right now and I'd hate to drag you in my mess."

"I'm willing to go there. Even if I have to get a little dirty." He bit his plump bottom lip and she tingled, both from the tempting invitation from Eddie and from the vibration of her phone. Surely it was Dante. "You already have me doing things I shouldn't be."

"Trust me, it's a lot more complicated than you think... I have to go." They both stood from their chairs and Eddie walked around his desk.

"When it's not complicated or still is and you just want me, call me." He softly slipped his card into her hands. "Or if you need more help with your sister. I'll keep you posted if I happen to find out anything."

"Thank you again." She slipped the card in her purse as he opened the door for her, her phone buzzing around for the second time. Sasha slipped her sunglasses back onto her face as she quickly exited the precinct. The driver opened the door and she slid inside to be met with an irritated Dante. "Sorry it took so long baby. I had to wait for him to finish up a call."

"Did he give you what I want?"

"Yes." The driver pulled off as she reached into her purse and handed him the paper slip with Cole's address on it.

"Where the hell is this?" Dante peered at the address before handing it to the driver upfront.

"He said it's in the Silverdale area, about an hour and half from here."

"Guess we have a little bit of a ride then." Dante placed a few cool cubes in a crystal glass and poured strong cognac inside. He took a long sip, feeling the burn of the alcohol as Sasha sparked up an L. "I wonder what led her there."

"Guess we'll find out..." Sasha side eyed him before taking a long pull. "Baby can I ask you a question?" She blew smoke and he nodded. "Since Nala ran away, I've been picking up the slack and doing a lot more than the other girls have. I cook for you, suck and fuck you anytime you want or when I want to And I'm helping you with this Nala business."

"Where was the question in all that Sasha?" She handed him the blunt and he puffed from it.

"When we find Nala, what's going to happen to me?"

"You'll still be here baby girl."

"Yea but as?" Dante looked over at her worried yet serious face as the smoke slowly spilled from his lips.

"What would you like to be?" He inquired as he moved closer to her and passed back the blunt.

"I want be your main woman." Sasha spoke up boldly. "I know I haven't been around as long the other girls, but my presence has been felt ever since I stepped inside that mansion. My loyalty already speaks volumes that surpasses their baby ass whispers of devotion to you. I don't see the rest of those bum bitches helping you out with anything and I only knew Nala for a couple days before she bounced on you. No disrespect to her but fuck her. She left, her loss. You already deal with enough maintaining the business. You don't need anybody who's gonna quit on you and damn sure don't need any leeches."

"So, tell me what I need then baby girl." Dante pulled Sasha on top of him, his hands disappearing under her dress to caress her backside.

"You need someone who compliments the strong, confident and sexy force you are." Sasha rubbed his chest with her free hand. "You need someone who's loyal to you. Someone you can trust to do whatever it takes to protect you and our home whether you're near or far. You need a rider. You need me." She kissed Dante's lips as slow and seductive as she could, feeling him rise and press up against her red lace thong. "Feels like you want me too." He smirked up at her as she took a pull from the blunt.

"You sure know what to say to a nigga." He'd never let her know it but for a moment there, she made him second guess his decision to track Nala down. Sasha was young and beautiful with the skin and body of a Godiva goddess. She was smart and loyal and had been following his lead ever since he let her inside the bedroom he shared with Nala. She matched his animalistic sexual appetite perfectly. He even liked the way she held her ground with the other girls. She was right, they'd be perfect together. But he needed Nala for more than what she or the other girls may have thought. "You don't ever have to worry about where you stand with me, I'ma always take care of you. Keep showing me you down and ridin' for me. I just might make your dreams of being my one and only come true." Sasha slyly grinned before pulling the thin straps of her dress down to reveal her breast. Dante began to lick them as she unbuckled his belt. She knew Dante would make all her dreams come true. To her, he didn't have any other option.

"Can we stop over and have breakfast with Bashi before we go?" Nala freed her wet curly from her towel as Cole pulled a white beater over his chest.

"Yea I think we got a little time." He looked over in time to watch Nala pull one of her new pair of jeans over her hips and button them, turning her waist about to see how they looked. She nodded her in satisfaction, happy to finally have something that fit her body. Nala caught Cole's eyes fixed on her waist and booty.

"What? You don't like them?" She looked down at the pants.

"No, they look great on you. My clothes didn't do you any justice." He complimented her and she blushed.

"Thanks." She continued to dress herself, Cole still admiring her as he slipped his shoes on. From the way her new jeans complimented her small waist and round booty to the way Lester's Given's mistress's white tank top fit comfortably over her torso and breast, he was finally able to fully see her beauty as a woman. He loved it. She caught him staring again and laughed. "What?"

"Hold on." Cole retrieved the duffle bag full of money and sat it on the dresser. Nala raised her brow as Cole unzipped the front pocket, looking over his shoulders as he did so. "Turn around and close your eyes." She squinted her eyes at him before doing so.

"You know the last time I had my back to you, I ended up with a gun butt to the head." She joked.

"Well hopefully this will make up for it." Cole placed the amethyst necklace in the middle of her chest and clasped it. Nala opened her eyes and stared down at the beautiful stone, speechless Cole had even come across something like it. "Let me see you." She turned around and he nodded at how perfect it looked on her. "You like it?" He looked into her awe filled eyes.

"Yes, it's beautiful." Nala finally spoke as she looked back down to the stone. Dante had always given her flawless diamonds and though they were amazing, they were nothing compared the sweet light purple gem. Simply because Cole gave it to her. "Thank you." She returned her eyes to him with a smile.

"You're welcome." He planted a kiss on her lips. She smiled up at him before giving him a softer, slower kiss. "You tryna start somethin' and we got moves to make." He laughed and shook his head as she pulled him closer.

"I'm not tryna do anything but thank you." She smiled and continued to thank him with her lips as he caressed and squeezed her backside. Cole's phone rang in his pocket and she groaned as he pulled away from her to answer.

"Good morning sir." Cole answered and smiled at her pouting face. "We were just about to head your way… Yea we'll be right over." Cole hung up and smooched Nala's lips once more. "I'm tryna tell you girl, you just got saved by Bashi."

"Gee thanks." Nala mumbled and continued to gather their few belongings.

"I don't know about the rest of you, but I'm ready for Dante's lap dog to get the fuck up outta here. I don't give a fuck what was said this morning. I don't trust that bitch." Natalia fanned herself as she and Paige lounged in the white cabana beside the enormous pool out back. Jade sat quietly by the cocaine white tiled pool with her feet in the cool water.

"Yea I definitely don't trust her. And the fact that Dante trust her enough to help him with whatever he has goin' on instead of one of us? The ones who've been here the longest besides Nala? Makes me think I shouldn't put my trust in him either." Paige sipped from her martini glass.

"Right! Like what makes her so special?" Natalia raised her brow. "We should just get rid of the bitch ourselves." Paige suggested.

"I'm down but how?" Natalia giggled.

"Let's drop the bitch off in the middle of the desert and make her walk till she passes out or tie boulders around her ankles and drop her in the ocean." They cackled loudly as Jade rolled her eyes underneath her dark designer shades and splashed her feet around in the water.

"Ooooh!!" Natalia sat up in her chair with excitement, "I could just call my crazy ass cousins to

211

come snatch her ass up. They'd have a ball with her before doin' away with the bitch."

"Y'all are heartless." Jade finally chimed in during Natalia and Paige's laughter. "Y'all that mad that this is what y'all are about to resort to? Murder?"

"Don't act like you don't want her gone just as much as we do. You're missin' out on Dante too." Natalia waved her off.

"Yea but I'm not bothered to point where I start plottin' to kill the girl. There's other ways around this."

"Sheesh, it was a joke. Loosen up a little." Paige laughed and nudged Natalia's arm as Jade removed her feet from the water and stood.

"Whatever, I'm going to go do something productive." She threw over her shoulder and walked off towards the house.

"Ugh, she's also starting to get on my fuckin' nerves." Natalia's eyes stayed on Jade's shrinking silhouette.

"Tell me about it." Paige shook her head.

"What's up her ass lately? She used to cut up with us and now all of a sudden, the bitch is quiet and boring. She walks around here all calm and cool like nothing bothers her. It's almost like she could care less what happens to us."

"You're right." Paige downed the rest of her glass. "She's comfortable...too comfortable."

"Maybe we should change that..."Natalia looked to Paige.

"Well this is a surprise." Bashi stood from his stool as Nala and Cole entered the restaurant with their possessions in hand. "Don't tell me you two are leaving m now?"

"Yea," Cole placed his duffle bag on one of tables as Bashi stepped down from behind the counter, "we decided it's best if we go ahead and get movin'."

"But do you all have a place to stay or a way to move around?"

"Somethin' like that." Cole looked to Nala.

"I don't like the way that sounds." Bashi folded his arms as his curious eyes danced back and forth between Nala and Cole.

"It's gettin' too hot to stay here and we don't want to drag you into any of our mess." Nala spoke up.

"No offense baby girl but I've been knee deep in mess before I even met you two." Bashi chuckled. "I really don't think it's a good idea for y'all to just be floatin' around out there either. Pick a place or make a goal point. Find a safe haven."

"We both don't have any family or friends to turn to."

"Yea so we're runnin' low on safe havens over here." Cole took a seat at the table and pulled Nala onto his lap.

"This place looks like shit." Sasha turned up her nose as the limo drove through the broken-down neighborhood, "You mean to tell me she left for this?" Sasha shook her head at Nala's choice of location. Dante furrowed his eyebrows as he scanned the dead and unfamiliar neighborhood. The limo slowed then came to a stop in front of a small dingy white house that was way overdue for a fresh coat of paint. There were two round medium sized bushes with very little green leaves on the parched branches and the outside windows were slightly tan from not being washed in so long.

"This it?" Dante asked.

"Yes sir." The driver confirmed. "Would you like me to go knock?"

"No." Dante adjusted his tie and notched a few buttons on his suit jacket, Sasha cringing on the inside at the sight of him fixing himself for Nala. "We can take care of this." Her demeanor softened at the sound of Dante including her. "Ready baby?" She nodded her head and Dante exited the limo to open her door for her. She stepped onto the cracked concrete and shut her door, taking in her surroundings. Sadly, the broken-down houses and dirty streets reminded her of her own rowdy upbringing. A life she swore she'd never return to. Dante had the means to keep her from that life; one of the many reasons she adored him. Dante turned the knob hoping that it was unlocked but no luck for him. He knocked hard on the door. No answer. He waited for some seconds before banging harder on the door but again, he was met with silence. Dante put his ear up to the door to listen for sounds of life

214

as Sasha continued to watch both ends of the street.

"Maybe she's sleeping. It's not even twelve yet."

"Let's wake her up then." Dante pulled his gun from inside his suit and shot around the knob and lock area, immediately pulverizing the wood.

"Y'all hear that?" Nala questioned during Bashi and Cole's deep conversation on the next moving point. They paused for a moment to listen out but shook their heads in confusion.

"Hear what?" Cole inquired.

"I don't know it was like loud crackling or a popping noise."

"That's prolly those fools out there gettin' started on today's shenanigans." Bashi shook his head again before he and Cole resumed their conversation. "What if you headed towards the direction of your grandmother?" Cole shrugged his shoulders as Nala kept her eyes glued to the front windows of the restaurant.

"I have been meaning to go see her... but I don't want to risk putting her in any danger. Besides, I don't know if they have someone watchin' the nursing home or any shit like that."

"Okay but I say you leave her open as an option." Bashi agreed. Sasha pushed open the door and stepped inside the living room, frowning at the sight of the poor furniture in the small house.

"At least the TV is halfway decent." Dante opened the door to the bedroom as Sasha went over the

215

kitchen. She opened the fridge to see some left-over food and half empty water bottles. She searched the cabinets to find a few plates and bowls but nothing else. Dante stepped inside the square bedroom, only a bare bed and dresser to greet him. He went through each of the drawers to find them spotless, slamming the last one in frustration. Sasha rolled her eyes at his slight temper tantrum and flicked on the light in the bathroom. It was just as clean as the bedroom, Dante unable to find anything in the closet either.

"Smart bitch." Sasha smirked to herself before turning the bathroom light off. "She isn't here baby."

"I can see that. You find anything?" They stood in the middle of the living room.

"Just some left over food." Sasha shook her head. "You?"

"Nothing. Nala left out so quickly I know she couldn't have gotten away with much. She wasn't holdin' any cash either, I made sure of that." After the first time Nala tried to run, he cut off her access to her own money and his as well. Anything she wanted, someone else had to pay for it. "Maybe she's had some help." Sasha thought back the number that had contact with Nala around the time she went missing.

"But who would help her? She has no one."

"What if I went and spoke to her for you?" Nala asked, finally taking her eyes off the front windows.

"That's not a bad idea." Bashi stood up to get a cup of coffee.

"I don't know La..." Cole hesitated and Nala began to play in his bush.

"She doesn't know me. I highly doubt anyone else around there does. Who knows, she might be able to point us in a new direction."

"That's somethin' I'm really gonna have to think about."

"Well one thing's for sure, someone lives here." Dante nodded.

"Okay so what do you want to do? Wait until that somebody walks through the door?" Sasha threw out sarcastically.

"Did you think we were doing somethin' else?" Dante took a seat on the hard couch and flipped on the TV with the remote that was laying on the coffee table. Sasha batted her eyes in disbelief.

"Dante, we could be here all day! And who's to say that she is actually here?"

"This is the address he gave you, isn't it?" Dante looked over at Sasha who was still standing in the middle of the cramped living room.

"Yes but-"

"Then we will wait until I feel I have all the answers I need."

"Only thing about going to see her is that we'd have to get through Adamson and that's a no-go zone for me." Cole shook his head. "They probably still have my picture hanging up at bus stops and grocery stores."

"I see your dilemma." Bashi returned to the table his coffee and paper. "How far is your grandmother past that?" Bashi inquired as he opened the paper and scanned the headlines.

"About an hour, hour and a half, I think? I can't remember, it's been a while since I've seen her." Cole hated to admit.

"Okay well I can't wait on an almost empty stomach." Sasha crossed her arms. Dante flipped the TV off and stood to his feet with a sigh.

"Spoiled ass. Come on."

"What about your little friend that you go out of town with? Think he can help you?" Bashi reminded Cole of Don. "If he can find work, I'm sure he can find a quiet place for you two to lay your heads."

"Damn I didn't think to ask him..." Cole didn't forget about Don, he just wasn't sure if he wanted Don to know about Nala. He knew Don would try and push the Bailey Estates job on her.

"Call him up and see if there's something he can do." Nala got off Cole's lap, allowing Cole to pull his cellphone out his pocket. She strolled over to the windows and began to wonder where Brittany was. Two days had passed without one sighting of her outside at all. Not even the junkie crew she runs with. Nala looked to right out the window to see the street quiet with no signs of life. To the left, she peered. Her next heartbeat was so strong and sudden, she could feel her pulse in her fingertips.

The glare of Dante's gold grilled black stretch limo began to brighten the closer the limo drove up the street.

"Dante's car is coming this way." She swiftly pulled away from the window.

"You need to disappear." Bashi began to pick up Nala and Cole's belongings to tuck them away behind the counter.

"For what?" Cole followed behind him.

"Because the best thing for us to do is protect her right now."

"By hidin' her? You know I wouldn't let anything happen to her."

"I know but we don't know who he's with or what his mentality will be if he happens to walk in here. Especially if he finds her in here with us. We protect ourselves to ensure her safety. We have to be smart." The bell sounded against the door.

"Hi there." A sweet voice called out to them. Bashi looked behind Cole to find a young woman in a small white dress smiling at him as a man in an all-black suit followed in behind her. Nala nowhere in sight.

"Well hello beautiful." He returned the smile and stepped down from the counter.

"Hope we weren't interrupting anything too important. We're not too familiar with this area. Dante." Dante reached for Bashi's hand.

"Bashi." He shook Dante's hand firmly. "And who might this pretty lady be?"

"Sasha." She smiled again and looked to Cole who was mum and lifeless in his expression.

"What brings you two round here? You looked dressed for a party and that sho' ain't happenin' round here." Bashi chuckled.

"We were going to visit a friend she doesn't seem to be home at the moment so we're hoping to find something to eat while we wait." Dante looked to Cole, who just so happened to be looking back at him.

"Well I do have a breakfast special I could whip up for ya. Eggs, bacon, pancakes and grits. It'll hit the spot."

"Sounds good." Dante returned his attention back to Bashi.

"That sounds great. I'm gonna head to the women's room and wash my hands babe." Sasha kissed Dante's lips. "I'm assuming it's back in this little hallway."

"You are right little lady." Sasha headed off to the bathroom, leaving the men to themselves.

"What'll it be to drink young man?"

"A coffee please." Sasha pushed open the door to the bathroom and frowned at pale yellow wallpaper. There were two dingy stalls with one sink that held a stack of paper towels. Sasha sighed and shook her head as she stared at herself in the spot filled mirror.

"This is fuckin' ridiculous," Sasha tossed her hair about in her hands, "we could be dining at the mansion or somewhere else, but he chooses this dump. All because he can't let go of her." Sasha paused as the sound of light hissing breath. She looked to the bottom of the stalls but saw not signs that anyone was using them. The sound of her heels clicking against the floor echoed as she walked to the first stall and opened the door. Empty. She pushed opened the door to the second and pleasant grin crossed her face.

"So, you must be Nala."

"I didn't catch your name brother." Dante looked to Cole before taking a seat the empty table close to the counter where Cole was standing.

"Cole."

"Aight Cole." Dante held out his hand to dap Cole up, but Cole remained unmoved from his spot at the front counter as Bashi placed a hot cup of coffee before Dante. Dante nodded before taking a sip from the mug.

"And you are?" Nala raised her brow at the girl as she sat on top of the commode.

"Someone you should be worried about."

"From the sound of it sweetheart, you're more worried about me than I am you."

"You from around here Cole?" Dante inquired as Bashi stood behind the grill preparing the breakfast he promised, looking over his shoulder at Cole each chance he could get. He knew Cole's pistol was tucked away on him somewhere.

"Guess you could say that. What about you?"

"Nah I'm from Black Mount."

"Black Mount huh? Explains the fancy suit, the limo and diamonds."

"What can I say," Dante looked down at the diamond rings on his pinky and middle fingers, "a nigga does well for himself."

"Trust me, if it weren't for Dante, you'd be at the bottom of the list of things to get out of my way but here we are."

"And again, honey, who are you?"

"Sasha. We didn't have a chance to really meet. You made your great escape not too long after I settled in the mansion."

"Black Mount is pretty far from here. What brings you to Silverdale?" Bashi questioned Dante.

"Looking for a friend. Haven't heard from her in a while so I figured I'd come check on her."

"She a junkie?" Bashi threw over his shoulder.

"No, no man, nothin' like that."

"Then whoever you lookin' for couldn't be here." Bashi laughed.

"I'm not too sure," Dante laughed along, "I was told she's here or has been here at least."

"She's supposed to be your friend, but you don't even know if she lives here?" Cole interjected.

"Sorry I couldn't stay to show you around the harem but as you can see, I had other plans." Nala stood to her feet.

"That's fine with me. The less of you I have to deal with, the better. You didn't happen to run off with that cute guy out there who doesn't know how to speak, did you?"

"No. And he talks, just to people he likes."

"Well I'm sure you two have had plenty to talk about." Sasha grinned. Dante looked between Bashi and Cole before chuckling and unbuttoning the last two buttons on his suit jacket.

"I'll be honest gentlemen. You see that girl I came in with? Legs smooth and long. Skin that taste like chocolate itself. And pussy so wet? Mm, makes you believe you're bathing under a waterfall. That tempting, desirable, sexy young lady I walked in with? She's mine."

"Sound like a lucky man." Cole finally sat down at the table.

"Oh yea, that's my best girl. Back in Black Mount I have more just like her. But it I've misplaced one of them so I'm trying to recover her."

"So, what now Sasha? I know Dante is out there. You gonna call him in so he can try and drag me outta here?"

"You know I think today I'm gonna do a great deed since I don't plan on doing many of them soon. Just for you Nala, I'll walk out of this bathroom, take Dante's hand and we'll both walk out of this raggedy ass restaurant. Then I'll take him back our mansion, fuck him til he sleeps for the rest of the day and we can pretend like none of this happened." Nala rolled her eyes.

"Glad somebody is willing to do it."

"Pretty soon I'll be the only one doing it." Sasha walked up to the mirror and checked her hair once more.

"So, if you have more girls at home, why trip off losin' this one?"

"She's special."

"Guess you should've taken better care of her then." Cole smirked and leaned back in his seat as Dante shots bullets at him with his eyes.

"Hopefully, you and I don't have to cross paths again. I doubt the next time would be this pleasant." Sasha turned to Nala.

"As much as it would satisfy my soul not to deal with anything related to Dante, I'm not stupid. I'm sure we'll meet again."

"Well then, I hope you'll be ready forwhatever's to come." Sasha smiled at her before exiting the bathroom. Dante and Cole remained in their silent stare down as Bashi tried to make small talk in the background while he flipped over pancakes. "Ya know, I expected place like this to be low grade but no paper towels?" Sasha complained as she rejoined them.

"My apologies Miss Sasha. I could've sworn I refilled them this morning." Bashi recalled as Dante stood to his feet.

"I think we're gonna go ahead and get movin'. I can see there's nothing of true value here." He looked down at Cole as he placed a hundred-dollar bill on the table. "But thank you for the meal anyway." He nodded graciously towards Bashi before taking Sasha's hand in to his.

"You should use that money you're not spending on paper towels to fix that broken toilet in the bathroom." Sasha winked at Bashi before Dante held open the restaurant door and they both disappeared. Cole walked over to the door and locked it as Dante looked back at the building with a smirk before getting in the limo and driving away.

"That went a lot smoother that what I could have imagined." Bashi sighed as he took a seat on his wooden stool.

"Yea too smooth." Cole made his way to the women's restroom to find Nala staring at herself in the mirror.

"No bloody nose or black eye? Either you and Dante made nice or he's gotten soft." She smiled at him through the reflection

"Now you of all people should know I'm not easy to take down." He walked up behind her placed his hands on her hips.

"I know." She rubbed his rough beard. "How was it?"

"Let's just say Dante and I won't be kickin' back havin' a few beers any time soon."

"Well the way Sasha came in here and professed her undying loyalty to Dante, it doesn't look like he'll be kickin' back with anybody here soon. Her crazy ass did buy us some time to get away though."

"Damn, you still wanna roll with me even though you got your "Get Away from Dante Free Card"?"

"Do you not want me to?" Nala turned to him with a puzzled expression.

"You got a way out from your own bullshit and from mine. The selfish part of me wants to keep you with me no matter what. Trust me I really do. But there's a part of me that cares about you Nala," he shook his head as he looked down into her confused eyes, "enough to not want you to come with me. There ain't no tellin' how my shit will end. I can't ask you to be a part of that."

"Someone once told me, "If you wanna go fast, go alone. If you wanna go far, go together."we don't have to get too heavy but I fuck with you Cole . "You didn't even know me, yet you were there for me without me asking and I appreciate it. I want to see how it ends with you."

"You sayin' you down to ride for me?" Cole wrapped his arms around her.

"Yea," she laced her fingers behind his neck, "I'm down to **ride**."